FATE

The California Obscura Series Book 4

ALEXA LAND

Contents

Most people believe supernatural creatures are the stuff of myths and fairy tales.

They're dead wrong.

How do I know? Because I'm part werewolf. While I don't have enough wolf in me to shift, the universe still saw fit to bind me for life to a fated mate—a domineering, remorseless criminal named Elias Reyes.

After spending the last century dodging him, Elias has finally tracked me down, and his timing couldn't be worse. He's managed to infuriate a pair of deadly demons, and they're closing in fast.

Will we manage to set aside our differences and unite against his enemies? Or will one of us get caught in the crossfire when Elias's past finally catches up to him?

Acknowledgments

Thank you **Anita, Kim, Melisha,** and **Kelly**
I truly appreciate your help and support!

Thank you as always to the members of Alexa's Land, my Facebook readers group, for your enthusiasm, encouragement, and friendship!

Cover Design by Alexa Land

Dedication

To Alan

Thanks for being one of the twelve

Chapter 1

Being part werewolf was a massive pain in the ass.

One thing I could really do without was my ridiculously acute sense of smell. It was making this run-down convenience store a real garden of delights, between the mold under the leaky cooler, the gallon of cheap cologne on the cashier, and the expired mystery meat hotdogs spinning in their greasy hot box.

My objective: get in, buy booze, and get out as fast as possible, but when I reached the wine section, I froze with indecision. I was shopping for my first date in decades and had no idea what was popular these days. After a few moments, I selected three different white wines and three reds. Then, just to be safe, I grabbed a rosé.

I hauled the armload of bottles up to the register, where the cologne-drenched cashier frowned at me and said, "Come on, kid. You look like you're barely eighteen."

"Not true. Most people think I'm in my mid-twenties."

He rolled his eyes. "Whatever. Let's see your ID."

Another annoying thing about being part werewolf—we aged very slowly, so even though I was pushing a hundred and twenty, I still regularly got carded. Since I was in a hurry, I waved my fingers and said, "You don't need to see my ID."

When he repeated, "I don't need to see your ID," and began ringing up my purchase, I couldn't help but grin. That Jedi mind trick was courtesy of my warlock side, which was a million times more fun and useful than that werewolf bullshit.

He packed the wine in a cardboard box with a picture of some sort of off-brand cereal mascot on the side. If it wasn't named Phony the Tiger, it should be. I loaded the alcohol in the trunk of my midnight blue Barracuda, and then I slid behind the wheel and took a deep breath.

On the drive back home, I tried to concentrate on calming the hell down. There was no reason to be nervous, since nothing was probably going to come of my date this evening. Sure, we'd seemed to click while chatting online, but it wouldn't take him long to realize I was odd and socially awkward once we were face-to-face. About the best I could hope for was that he'd fuck me anyway before never calling me again.

As I turned onto the private driveway leading to my home, I tried to imagine how this place would look to my date. The security gate had been torn off its hinges by a friendly but impatient vampire a few months ago, and it was leaning against the retaining wall. That would probably raise some questions.

So would the fact that I lived in a huge, purple Victorian, which seemed wildly out of place in the Hollywood Hills. It looked sinister in the dark, so when I reached the top of the driveway, I flicked my fingers and turned on all the exterior lights. Now it just looked like an overgrown dollhouse. In retrospect, I really should have made plans to meet him anywhere but here.

I parked off to the side to make room for my guest, then lugged my wine haul up the stairs and through to the kitchen at the back of the house. Now the waiting game began.

I'd expected him at eight, and when he still hadn't arrived by eight-fifteen, I was sure I was being stood up. I picked up my phone five or six times with the intention of messaging him to see if he was on his way, but I kept putting it down again without sending a text. If he wasn't coming I'd know soon enough, and I didn't really want to hear whatever flimsy excuse he came up with for ditching me.

Finally, at nineteen past the hour, I heard a car coming up the driveway and dashed into the nearest bathroom to quickly assess my reflection. I'd just gotten a haircut, and my black hair was very short on the sides. Maybe too short. I tried to finger-comb the longer bit at the top as I frowned at my outfit. I'd gone with a light blue button-down shirt and jeans, and that wardrobe choice wasn't doing me any favors. No wonder I'd gotten carded. I looked like a high school senior who'd dressed up for picture day.

After doing what I could with my hair, I hurried to the front of the house. Meanwhile, my date had reached the top of the driveway, and he cut the engine. The moment he stepped out of the car, I caught his scent and paused.

By coincidence, he was part warlock, but there were other elements there, too. Selkie, maybe? Or fae? It all came together in a way that was both interesting and appealing.

But now the question became, did he know he was anything other than human? It wasn't all that unusual to encounter people with a bit of nonhuman blood in them. After all, the different subspecies had been interbreeding for centuries. But these days, mainstream society wrote off paranormal creatures as myths and fairy tales, even though the real story flowed through a lot of people's veins.

The wards on the house were set to block nonhuman strangers, so I ran to the front door and threw it open before he bounced off the invisible wall at the foot of the stairs. Shit like that tended to raise a lot of questions.

The guy in my driveway was beautiful. He'd sent a photo while we'd been chatting online and I remembered thinking he was cute, but he was actually much more than that. He was tall, willowy, and graceful, with slightly overgrown golden-blond hair that probably always looked tousled, even if he tried to style it. Even though he was dressed casually in jeans, a dark blue T-shirt, and a leather jacket, there was an elegance and sophistication about him. It was easy to imagine him as a ballet dancer, or something along those lines. Since he'd told me he was a programmer during our chats, it seemed he'd really missed his calling.

As he ran a hand over my car's shiny fender, I called, "Hey, you must be Logan. I'm Matt." Nobody ever called me that. My name was actually Mateo, but I'd thought it would be smart to maintain a bit of anonymity on the dating site where we'd met.

"It's nice to finally meet you, Matt," he called. "Your Barracuda is a thing of beauty."

I was nervous as hell, and I wiped my sweaty palms on my jeans as I walked down the stairs. "Thanks. She was in pretty rough shape when she came to me, and restoring her has been a lot of fun."

We'd initially bonded over our mutual obsession with 1960s and 70s muscle cars, so it wasn't surprising that he seemed more interested in my Cuda than me. But then he turned to me and flashed a friendly smile. Right about then, I realized I couldn't read his mind. That was rare, but it happened now and then with certain nonhumans.

He was maybe six-one to my five-foot-nine, and I looked up into inquisitive brown eyes. "You've done an amazing job," he said. "I keep saying I'm going to restore my car, but I barely know where to start."

I turned to look at his sky blue 1970 Trans Am and said, "It seems to be all original and in pretty decent shape, so my advice is not to go too crazy with the restoration. Sometimes it's nice to just appreciate a thing for what it is, instead of wishing it was something different."

When I turned back to him, there was a lull in the conversation as we studied each other. He really was handsome. In fact, he was drastically out of my league. Finally, I remembered my manners and blurted, "Would you like to come inside?" Duh. What else were we going to do, stand in the driveway?

"Sure. Just a minute." When he walked back to his car, I half-expected him to climb in and speed away to escape from my awkwardness. Instead, he reached through the open passenger window and retrieved a bottle of wine.

He returned to my side and handed it to me, and I glanced at the label and said, "Thanks, this was really thoughtful." That single bottle of merlot had probably cost more than my entire wine haul, which made me feel like a cheapskate.

As we headed toward the house, I sent out a silent incantation to tell the wards he was a friend, and it was okay to let him in. He followed me up the stairs, and I asked, "Did you have any trouble finding the place?" God, I sucked at small talk. What was I going to ask him next, whether he came here often?

"No, your directions were perfect. Sorry I'm late, by the way. I underestimated traffic, which has to be the worst excuse any Angelino can ever come up with."

"It happens, so no worries."

He glanced at the two dozen garden gnomes clustered beside the front door and asked, "Is this your house?"

"No. I live here and look after it, but it actually belongs to a friend of mine. The gnome convention is my doing, though. They were scattered all around the landscaping, and this week I decided to gather them up and relocate them to the backyard. Just to, you know, make the place seem a little more normal."

"I see."

He definitely didn't see and was probably starting to realize just how awkward I was. I barreled ahead with, "My friend Griffin inherited this place from his aunt and didn't have the heart to change anything after she died, so brace yourself. The inside is even frillier and more eccentric than the outside, and the purple continues throughout most of the house. That's it for the gnomes, though."

When we reached the foyer, Logan glanced at the living room on our left, which was a feminine, floral, Easter egg-colored nightmare. "The lady in the portrait above the fireplace is my friend's Aunt Roz, who left him this place," I said, not that he asked. "She was a film star in the forties and fifties, and this house was her pride and joy."

"It's a beautiful home."

"It is for sure," I said. "But it's probably not what you were expecting."

"I'm not sure what I was expecting, but I like this place," he said. "It's interesting." Interesting was one of those words that could definitely be interpreted more than one way. He probably meant it was so fucking weird that he'd be talking about it with his buddies for weeks to come.

When we reached the lavender kitchen, I pulled two wine glasses from the cupboard while he wandered around looking at all the silly little tchotchkes lining the shelves and counters. After a moment, he asked, "Is your friend Griffin home?"

"No. He and his husband are on an extended honeymoon in Paris."

"So, you're all by yourself in this huge house?"

"Yeah, but that's nothing new. They actually spend most of their time at their second home in the desert."

He said, "You must get lonely."

Since I was trying not to come across as pathetic, I pulled up a smile and told him, "I'm used to being by myself."

After I poured two glasses of the merlot he'd brought, Logan asked, "Can we sit outside? It's a nice night." When I agreed, he followed me through the den, then out a pair of French doors to the patio.

He was right about it being nice out. It was fairly warm for mid-March, and the moon was nearly full. As we settled onto a pair of Adirondack chairs, he said, "I noticed your slight accent. Where are you from?"

"I was born in Mexico, but I moved to the U.S. just before my twentieth birthday."

"Did your family come with you?"

That question hurt a lot more than it should have, and I muttered, "I don't have a family." After a moment, I amended that with, "Well, that's not true. Griffin's my family, even if we're not related by blood."

Logan asked, "How'd you two meet?"

I drank some wine while I thought about what to say. The real answer was that I'd been best friends with his mom. She and her husband had been killed when Griffin was a baby, and I'd been looking out for him ever since. But I just left it at, "Through a mutual friend."

"Is he part werewolf, too?" I turned to him with a look of surprise, and he said, "I know we're not supposed to blurt that out, because most people have no idea the paranormal world exists. But I can sense you're only half human with a lot of werewolf and warlock blood, so you must know the truth."

"I'm glad you said something. It's tough, never knowing who we can open up to. And to answer your question, no, Griffin isn't part wolf." He was actually something extremely rare, a full-blooded warlock, but that information had to be kept secret for his safety. Power like his tended to attract attention, usually from people who either wanted to exploit or destroy it. That was what had gotten Griffin's parents killed.

I glanced at Logan's profile and asked, "What are you? I detect a bit of warlock, but the rest is a jumble."

"I'm a lot of things, with just enough warlock blood to be able to do this." He grinned at me as he pantomimed throwing a ball.

For a few glorious moments, the sky lit up with fireworks. I laughed delightedly, but then I said, "You should be careful. You know how important it is for our kind to stay hidden."

He shrugged. "Anyone who saw that would just assume a human was playing with illegal fireworks."

"Still, though."

"Sorry. I thought you'd find it romantic." Logan studied me in the soft glow of the patio light, and after a moment he asked, "Don't you ever cut loose, do things you know you shouldn't?"

"No, not really."

"Why not?"

"I guess I prefer staying in my comfort zone," I said. "Actually, I live a pretty simple life. All I ever do is work on cars and watch telenovelas, and I don't go out much, aside from an occasional run to the market or liquor store. The reason I asked you to come here for our date is because I feel safest at home, and it was less intimidating than meeting you at a bar or restaurant." I drained my glass before muttering, "I must sound ridiculous."

"No. You sound honest."

I stood up and said, "You're just being nice. I know I'm a mess, and if you want to leave, I totally understand."

Logan placed his glass on the arm of his chair and got up, too. "I'm actually having a nice time." He came closer and ran his hands down my upper arms. "I like you, Matt."

"It's actually Mateo."

"That's a beautiful name." When I looked up at him, he studied me for a few moments, and then he started to lean in for a kiss. My breath caught, and I stepped back quickly. "I'm sorry," he said. "Was that too soon?"

"It's more than that. I thought I could do this. I really wanted to. You're so nice, but I just…can't."

"Why not?"

"Because there's someone else."

He asked, "You're married?" I shook my head. "So, you have a boyfriend."

"No."

"You don't mean you have a mate, do you? Because from what I've heard about werewolves, that's pretty rare."

I sighed and admitted, "Unfortunately, that's exactly what I mean."

Logan asked, "Does he know you're dating?"

"I don't date. Not really. It's been years since I tried, and if he knew what I was doing right now, he'd be furious. Like all alphas, he's extremely territorial."

"So, can I expect him to hunt me down and beat me up?"

"No. I actually haven't seen him in a century," I said. "In fact, I don't even know if he's in California anymore. I refused our bond when we met and have been hiding from him ever since."

"I didn't think fated mates could do that."

"It's not easy. Most don't even try." I looked up at him and said, "I'm so sorry. It must seem like I led you on by inviting you here. But I thought maybe this time I could go through with it, because so much time had passed. I feel too guilty, though. Even if I don't want to be with my mate, I'm still—"

"His." I sighed and looked away, but then I nodded. "It's okay, I get it. Maybe I should go, considering the circumstances." I followed him through the house, and when we reached the front door, he turned to me and said, "I hope things work out for you."

On impulse, I grabbed him in a hug. Logan seemed startled and his posture went rigid, but after a few seconds, I felt him relax. He put his arms around me and held me for a long moment, until I finally stepped back and murmured, "Thanks for being so understanding."

"Maybe someday you'll find a way to be free of him once and for all, and maybe we'll see each other again. You never know. Until then, take care of yourself, Mateo."

I watched him as he walked out the door and down the stairs, and I felt it as the invisible wards around the house snapped shut behind him. He climbed into his car and fired up the engine, then swung around in a wide arc and took off down the long, winding driveway.

The house was so quiet in his wake.

Too quiet.

I trudged to the den, grabbing the bottle of merlot along the way. After I pushed off my shoes, I curled up in a little ball under my favorite blanket, which was old, ratty, and comforting. Then I used the remote to pull up one of the telenovelas recorded on my DVR.

I drank from the bottle and stared unseeingly at the TV screen for a while. There was a dull ache in my chest, one that just wouldn't go away, and I whispered, "Damn it."

I really thought I'd made my peace with being lonely. There'd been entire decades when I'd tolerated it just fine. But when my best —and only—friend got married and moved to the desert with his beautiful husband, he left a huge void in his wake. Then that familiar feeling of loneliness became something bigger, something I couldn't really control. I hated that.

With a sigh, I got up and opened another bottle of wine.

I ended up dozing off on the couch, which was nothing new. I slept there most nights anyway. But I awoke a few hours later with the hair on the back of my neck standing on end. Just as I was trying to figure out what woke me, the power cut out, plunging the house into darkness.

I slipped out from under the blanket and moved to the center of the room. A perk of being part werewolf was that I could see perfectly in the dark, and nothing seemed out of place. But there was a feeling in the air, something electric, and I exhaled slowly, then closed my eyes and reached out with my senses.

What I found sent a trickle of fear down my spine. There was something in the driveway, something dark and powerful. It was working systematically to attack the wards that protected my home —and me.

My heart began to race. I ran into the kitchen and picked up the land line, but it was dead. So was my cellphone, which I found on the counter. Great, so I was totally cut off.

I took a breath and focused on the thing outside. When I tried to read its thoughts, all I got was the chant it was repeating in a language I didn't understand, which was battering the wards like a giant hammer.

Was it here for Griffin? Power like his tended to attract attention. Or maybe it was after his husband Ari, who was a fallen angel with some pretty formidable enemies. I'd worked with Griffin to make this home a fortress, but right now I wasn't sure if our combined magic was any match for whatever was outside.

I wasn't powerful enough to use my magic at a distance, so I ran to the front of the house, gathering as much energy as I could along the way. When I reached the foyer, I pushed both hands out in front of me. The burst of energy I directed at the thing in the driveway didn't even sort of disrupt it.

I reached out to try to read its thoughts again and got a lot of noise, in a form I'd never heard before. It was fascinating, and for just a moment I considered opening the front door to take a look at it. The door itself wasn't what was keeping it out anyway. What was holding it back was an energy barrier—and it was starting to weaken.

A thought appeared in my head that didn't belong to me. It said, "You're right, Mateo, the door's not protecting you anyway. Why don't you open it and say hello?" That was coming from the dark, inhuman thing in the driveway. I was sure of it.

"Who are you?" I said that out loud, but I could have just thought it, and the entity still would have heard me.

"A friend of a friend."

"Be more specific. What friend?" He tried to hide it from me, but I caught a glimpse of the name before he locked it down. I blurted, "For fuck's sake, Elias Reyes sent you? Are you kidding me? This is happening because of my fucking mate?"

Just then, a wave of energy slammed into the front of the house and made it shake. I swore vividly and bolted down the hall with the plan of climbing the back fence and running away.

Another wave shook the Victorian, strong enough to make the dishes rattle in the cabinets. The thing in my driveway was going with a new strategy, slamming the wards at a single point instead of trying to take them all down, and it was working awfully well.

By the time I got my shoes on—which probably took all of four seconds—another wave of energy slammed into the spot at the front of the house. For just a moment, the world outside my windows flared with blue light before plunging into darkness again.

The wards protecting the house were about to fail.

The next wave of energy knocked me to the floor. I scrambled to my feet and rushed for the back door as my heart pounded in my ears. When I tried to run outside, an impenetrable wall of energy shoved me back. Damn it, whatever it was had put up wards of its own to keep me in.

Another huge wave of energy knocked me off my feet again. Then everything went eerily still.

I took a shaky breath as fear cascaded through me like ice water. The thing was in the house. I could feel it.

But it wasn't coming for me. What was it waiting for?

Since I was trapped, I decided the only thing I could really do was go and confront whatever it was. I took a deep breath, balled up my fists, and went to face off against the intruder.

When I reached the foyer, all the lights came on at once, and I found it sitting in my frilly, pastel living room. He'd chosen to take human form, and he was big and muscular with dark hair, pale gray eyes, and a smirk that seemed right at home on his handsome face. With his impeccable black-on-black suit, shirt, and tie, he seemed to be going for some sort of supernatural mafioso thing.

He smiled at me and said, "Mateo Figueroa, I presume."

"Who are you?"

"You can call me Carter."

"And you're what, exactly?" The dark energy radiating from him was stunningly powerful, and I didn't detect even a drop of human blood in him.

"We'll get to that later. For now, you need to come with me."

"So you can deliver me to Elias? Fuck that."

"You've kept him waiting long enough," he said. "A century without you has torn him to shreds, metaphorically speaking."

"Since you're basically Oz the Great and Powerful, why don't you just break the mate bond, so he can get on with his life?"

Carter stood up and adjusted his cuffs as he said, "The only thing that can break a mate bond is death. You know that as well as I do. Besides, he doesn't want the bond broken. He wants you."

He took a step forward, and I backed up until I bumped into the wall. I started to gather my energy so I could hit him with every-thing I had left, and blue light sparked and crackled around my fingertips as I told him, "There's no way in hell I'm going anywhere with you."

He seemed genuinely amused. "As if you have a choice."

When he snapped his fingers, unconsciousness slammed into me from every angle. The last thing I remembered was the creature in a man suit catching me before I hit the floor.

Chapter 2

I woke with a start and drew a sharp breath. It was more than a little alarming to discover I was on a private jet, and we were in the air.

A blanket slid off me and onto the floor as I sat up. Carter was seated a few feet away, reading a newspaper. I probably should have been afraid of him, given the fact that he was some type of dark entity who'd abducted me. But right now, his presence read not only as nonthreatening but soothing, which probably meant he'd cast some kind of spell. I was still wary of him, because I wasn't a total idiot.

I asked, "Where are we going?"

He looked up from his paper. "To Elias, of course."

"And he's where, exactly?"

"You'll see."

When I tried to read his thoughts, I discovered he'd put up some sort of wall to totally keep me out. I sighed and pulled the blanket back onto my lap before asking, "What's the point in keeping that information from me? You already succeeded in kidnapping me, and now we're on a plane. If you tell me we're on our way to

France, or Guadalajara, or Detroit, what could I possibly do with that information?"

"Let's not find out."

A long pause stretched between us. When I realized no additional information would be forthcoming, I asked, "Why did Elias send you to get me, instead of coming for me himself?"

"He got in a bit of trouble back in December and had to leave L.A. in a hurry. On his way to the airport, he sensed your presence, but only for a moment. He didn't want to leave without you, but staying would have cost him his life. The only way to get him to go was to promise I'd find you myself, which ended up taking three months."

"I have no idea how you tracked me down," I muttered.

"It wasn't easy, until you set off those magical fireworks earlier tonight. You might as well have hired a skywriter to write your name and draw a huge arrow in the sky, pointing to your house. Not that I'm complaining, of course. Searching for you had grown tiresome on day two."

"I didn't set off the fireworks."

"Well, they still led me to you. I'd been investigating any and every magical occurrence in L.A., on the off chance you were behind it."

"But how did you determine where they came from? The fireworks covered a huge area," I said.

"All magic leaves a trace. Theirs pointed at your house like a beacon."

I studied him for a few moments before asking, "Why would someone as ridiculously powerful as you choose to work for a part werewolf, two-bit criminal like Elias Reyes?"

"I don't work for him, or anyone else."

"Then why are you helping him?"

"Because he's my friend."

"Bullshit," I said. "Elias doesn't have friends."

"Not many, it's true, but he has me."

"You could do better."

"And you could do so much worse for a mate."

"You know, he and I spent some time together when our bond first activated," I said. "But we just aren't compatible, no matter what kind of totally involuntary attraction happens when we're near each other."

"You didn't give him a chance."

"Sure I did, and during our time together he was rude, domineering, and cold as ice. Plus, I want someone who loves me for who I am, not because they're under the influence of some weird cocktail of magic, lust, and pheromones."

Carter frowned and said, "You only spent three days with him, and then you ran. You didn't even consummate your relationship. If you had, your bond would have been complete and you'd both be happy."

"I couldn't sleep with him."

"Why not?"

I held his gaze and said, "Let me ask you something, just hypothetically. Let's say you go to a bar and meet a beautiful girl."

"If it's all the same to you, I'd prefer a boy."

"Alright, a beautiful boy. He's just your type, but he's also drunk off his ass. Do you take him home and fuck him?"

Carter looked appalled. "Of course not!"

"Why not?"

"Because if he's drunk he's not able to give consent, so it would be deplorable to take advantage of him."

I leaned forward and told him, "When I'm with Elias, it's the same as being drunk. I'm under the influence of that aforementioned cocktail of magic and pheromones and whatever else is in the mix, and I don't have the ability to think clearly. I'm obviously not suggesting Elias would force himself on me. I'm just trying to explain that I'm not in control of myself when we're close to each other and the mate bond is activated. So, you're about to put me in a situation where I'm unable to give consent, Carter."

Despite whatever he'd done to lock me out of his thoughts, I felt the conflict in him. It seemed Carter had principles, and I'd struck a nerve. After a pause, he said, "I have to think about this. Please don't do anything stupid while I'm gone." What was I going to do, crash the plane out of spite? That wouldn't exactly work to my advantage. He got up and went into the cockpit, closing the door behind him.

I exhaled slowly, then shifted around so I was leaning against the arm of the couch and looked out the window. The sun was just beginning to rise. By its position, I could tell we were heading in a more or less northeastern direction, but that didn't narrow down our destination by much.

Maybe fifteen minutes passed before Carter returned to his seat. He studied me with a troubled expression as he said, "I never thought about it like that before, but you're right. If you and Elias are both under the influence of your mate bond, neither of you can give consent."

"Exactly. That's why you need to let me go."

"That won't solve my friend's problem. He needs some sort of closure where you're concerned."

"If your solution is to break the bond by killing me, I don't consent to that, either."

"I'm not going to hurt you."

"Yeah, probably not. You actually seem like a pretty decent guy, aside from the whole breaking into my house and kidnapping me thing. Then again, I don't really know you, do I? In fact, I don't even know what you are, or if Carter is your first or last name."

"It's my only name, though not my original one, and I'm a demon. That's why I couldn't just walk up and knock on your door. Your wards were set to automatically lock out anything that reads as evil."

"Interesting. I've never met a demon before."

He seemed surprised. "No hysterics? No unflattering assumptions about my kind?"

"There's a lot of darkness in you. Truly staggering amounts, actually. But I believe we all should get to decide who we want to be, no matter what cards we're dealt. The fact that you're trying so hard to help your friend says a lot about the choices you've made."

He asked, "Why are you so quick to give a total stranger—and a demon, at that—the benefit of the doubt, but you won't do the same for your mate?"

"Because I know him, and there's no warmth or compassion in Elias."

"Sure there is," he insisted. "You'll see."

"So, you're going through with your plan of taking me to him." When he nodded, I asked, "Did that earlier conversation about consent mean nothing to you?"

"It meant everything to me. That's why I'm planning to suppress your bond before I leave you with him."

"You can do that?"

"I think so, but it won't be easy. Mate bonds are extremely powerful. This can only be a short-term thing, because it'll require constant effort and energy on my part. My goal is to keep it contained for a week. That should be plenty of time for you and Elias to get to know each other without any distractions."

"I'll mean nothing to him without the bond. What if he tries to hurt me?"

"He wouldn't do that. Also, you're hardly defenseless," Carter said. "He might be strong, but he doesn't have any magical ability, while you're surprisingly formidable."

"Does he know what you're planning?"

"No, and I think he'll probably be furious with me. I won't be able to suppress the bond until we're together, and that means he'll be deep in its thrall when we first arrive. It might be a shock to his system when it cuts out abruptly."

"Assuming you're even able to block it," I said.

"I've learned a few tricks over the years. I'm pretty sure I can do this."

I thought about it before saying, "I like the idea of getting to talk to Elias when we're both sober, for lack of a better word. It might be pointless in the long run, because as soon as the bond returns it'll just override everything again. But I think he needs this. I've been able to resist our bond and stay away from him all these years, and once he realizes we're totally wrong for each other, hopefully he'll be able to do the same."

Carter frowned and muttered, "That's hardly the result I'm hoping for."

"Well, if you're expecting us to fall in love for real without the bond's influence and live happily ever after, you're going to be disappointed. I don't want this! I never asked for a mate, and I never chose Elias."

"No one gets to choose who they fall in love with, kid."

I said, "I'm almost a hundred and twenty. Don't call me a kid."

"Apologies. But did you hear what I said? *No one gets to choose who they fall in love with.* It just happens, and the people involved have absolutely no control over it. So, your mate bond sprang to life automatically when you turned twenty, and you didn't get to select your partner. So what? You've been given the rarest and most precious gift imaginable, a soul mate, and you've totally failed to appreciate it or show the slightest bit of gratitude."

"Gratitude. Right. You're trying to convince me having no choice and no freedom is somehow a good thing, but come on, Carter. You're a demon overflowing with dark energy, but you're choosing not to be evil. In other words, you didn't just accept what the universe handed you without question, but somehow you're expecting me to."

He shook his head. "You can't compare the two. I'm asking you to say yes to love, and you're talking about the choice I make every single day not to burn down the world."

I stared at him and asked, "Metaphorically speaking? Or could you really burn it down?"

"I could put a pretty big dent in it."

"Can I see your true form? Is it terrifying? I assume the idea of horns and a red complexion is just bullshit, but man would I love to see the real you."

Carter frowned at me. "Are you trying to make me angry? Just so you know, that's not a great idea."

"No, I'm not. I just want to stop talking about how lucky I am to have no say whatsoever in who I ended up with as my mate."

"At least you have a mate," he said. "I'm one of only three demons on earth, and believe me when I say the other two are something from your worst nightmares. There's literally no one for me here while you have a wonderful man who'd do anything for you, and you're treating him like a rash you can't wait to get rid of."

"Is there some reason you can only date other demons?"

"What do you mean?"

"You just told me there are only two other demons on earth, so there's no one for you to pair up with," I said. "Is dating another demon a requirement of some kind?"

"No, it's not. But who else besides another demon would be willing to take a chance on someone like me?"

"Lots of people. Elias, maybe, if he wasn't saddled with me." I watched him closely as I asked, "Are you in love with him?"

"No. Why do you ask?"

"Because you've spent the last three months doing a favor for him, and that suggests far more than a friendship."

"That's no time at all when you've lived as long as I have," Carter said. "And I was willing to do it because I care about him and want him to be happy."

"Why does he mean so much to you?"

"He was there for me when I needed a friend. It's as simple as that."

I asked, "What's he like with you? Is he warm and friendly? Kind and thoughtful? Does he seem to care about your feelings and show a real interest in your life?"

"You won't believe me if I tell you he's all of those things, so just wait and see what he's like for yourself."

"I already know what he's like."

"You gave him *three days*. I can't believe that's all the time you spent with him when you two first met," he said.

"He was horrible during that time. He ordered me around, treated me like a possession, and tried to take control of my entire life."

"Well, he is your alpha, which means he was just doing his job." I rolled my eyes. The steady hum of the jet engine changed slightly, and Carter glanced out the window as he murmured, "Looks like we're beginning our descent into Belfast."

"Ireland?"

"Maine."

"What are we doing here?"

"Trading the jet for a helicopter."

"Then what?"

"Then," he said cheerfully, "I'm delivering you to your one true love." All I could do was sigh.

Chapter 3

Maybe twenty minutes later, we landed at a small municipal airport. Surprisingly, Carter had actually thought to pluck one of my coats off the rack by the front door when he was abducting me, and I put it on before following him out of the plane.

It was bitterly cold. Even though I appreciated the coat, it had been bought for Southern California winters and didn't really stand a chance of keeping me warm in Maine. We hurried across the tarmac, and Carter reached a sleek, black helicopter a moment before me and opened the door.

I forgot about the cold when a faint but all-too-familiar scent slammed into me, and I blurted, "You didn't tell me Elias was at the airport."

"He's not. If you just picked up his scent, it's because this is his helicopter and he's flown it in the past. Lately, it's been used by an assistant to bring him supplies."

I asked, "Can you suppress my side of the mate bond now? It's already affecting me, and I need to be clear-headed when I see him."

"No. I don't want to attempt anything until you two are together and the bond is fully activated."

This was going to suck.

I reluctantly boarded the helicopter, and Carter began his pre-flight check while I wrapped my arms around myself, pressed my eyes shut, and tried to ignore the scent that felt like it was seeping into my pores. After a few minutes, he handed me a pair of head-phones and put on a matching pair, and then he started the over-head rotors.

Once we took off, he headed out over the ocean. "Um, land is in the other direction," I said, through the headphones.

"I know. Elias lives on an island."

I imagined someplace like Catalina, an island off the coast of California with a population of around four thousand people. We flew over an island kind of like that, but then we kept going. Every now and then, more islands would appear below us in the steel gray sea. When we passed another with a small town on it, I asked, "Out of curiosity, how many people live on Elias's island?"

"That number fluctuates."

"Give me a ballpark idea."

"I don't think I should."

"Why not?"

"Because you won't like the answer."

"Just tell me," I said. "It's better than finding out when we get there."

He hesitated before admitting, "There's usually a population of one."

"One? He's the only person on the entire fucking island?"

"The population is about to double in size. Told you it fluctuated."

"No, forget it. I'm not doing this."

"Why not?"

"Because this isn't what I signed up for," I said. "Spending time with him was one thing. Doing it while trapped on an island in the middle of the ocean is another thing entirely."

"It's not in the middle of the ocean. In fact, we'll be there in just a few minutes."

"If I decide to leave, how do I do that? Because I don't trust you to come running with the helicopter if I call you."

"There's a boat," he told me. "You won't be stuck there."

"How big is this island?"

"It's…small."

My voice rose. "How small, Carter?"

"I don't know, exactly. Maybe a quarter mile long and half as wide?"

"Nope. I can't be stuck on a tiny island with him for a whole week, even without the bond. Turn the helicopter around."

He sighed and told me, "I'm not turning around, Mateo. You can give Elias a week, after dodging him for the last century. And if you get really desperate to leave, like I said, there's a boat."

"I don't like this. It feels like I'm walking into a trap."

"You're not. This is just where he's been staying for the last three months. It wasn't selected to keep you trapped or isolated." He gestured ahead of us and said, "Look, there it is. I'll circle around before we land, so you can see the whole thing."

Directly ahead of us, a scattering of tiny islets rose from the choppy sea. Most held nothing but vegetation. The biggest of the lot was covered in pine trees and ringed by a rocky shore, with a pier and a weather-beaten boathouse at one end. The right half of the island rose in a gradual slope from the water's edge, and in a clearing at its peak sat a dark, gothic Edwardian, which clashed with the modern helipad in the field behind it.

Carter did a lap around the entire island, which took a few seconds. As we approached the helipad, a tall figure dressed all in black appeared at the back of the house. My heart started racing as I asked, "Did Elias know we were coming?"

"Yes. I called him before we left L.A."

"He actually has a phone that works out here?"

"It's a satellite phone."

I turned to Carter, as much as I could with the seatbelt pinning me down, and said, "Please don't just abandon me here. Promise you'll come back in a week, and promise me you really will suppress the bond."

"I swear on my life I'll do all of that, and I'll make sure you're alright."

For some reason, I believed him. "Okay," I said. "I'll give him a week, because I figure I owe Elias one more chance, after avoiding him for a century. This is it, though. If we can't make it work this time, there's no hope for us."

Once we touched down and Carter cut the engine, I took off my headphones and muttered, "Shit, he's coming." I fumbled with my seatbelt, got it unfastened, and tumbled out the door moments before Elias reached the helipad. As he strode toward me, I stumbled backwards.

The strong breeze was carrying his scent directly to me, and it overpowered my senses. Every part of me responded. My god, he was beautiful—so beautiful I almost couldn't stand it. He was perfect. He was everything. A whimper, more wolf than human, slipped from me as I fell to my knees. I needed him to fuck me right then and there, and—

No. *No.*

That was the bond talking. It had almost wiped out all my rational thought in a matter of seconds. How had I resisted him for three whole days last time?

Before Elias reached me, Carter stepped between us and stopped him with a hand on his chest. Then the demon guided him a few feet away and told him our plan. It looked like he handed Elias something at one point, but I couldn't be sure about that.

While they were talking, I stood up and repositioned myself so I wasn't directly downwind of Elias. It helped a little to not be bombarded by his scent, and as my head cleared, I studied my mate.

At six-foot-two, he had a solid five inches on me, along with a powerful, muscular build. He looked like he was in his early thirties, although he was actually pushing two hundred. And he was absolutely stunning, with chiseled features, dark eyes, and thick, black hair that grazed his collar. I wondered if he'd still seem as gorgeous once the mate bond released its hold on me.

When Carter finished explaining the logic behind suppressing our bond, Elias snapped, "Absolutely not."

"Why not?"

"Because he's my mate! We're meant to be bonded. There's no point in wiping it away for a week to see if we get along without it."

Carter said, "Do it for Mateo. Show him he can trust you, and take the time to get to know him. I realize the bond's going to override everything else when it returns, but this is important to him."

"I just spent the last century without my mate," Elias told him, "all because he was too stubborn and willful to accept the inevitable. Now we're finally together again, and the first thing you want to do is tamper with our bond. That's bullshit, and I'm not doing it."

"I won't force this on you," Carter said, "but I'm also not going to force Mateo to stay here against his will. You have two choices, Elias—accept this or say goodbye, because I'm prepared to take him back to the mainland."

Elias exclaimed, "That's no choice at all!"

Carter looked apologetic as he shrugged, in a gesture that tried to suggest this was beyond his control. "Take it or leave it."

Elias ground his teeth for a long moment before snapping, "Fine. Do it now, before I change my mind."

Carter held his hand out to me, and I hurried to his side and took it. He knit his brows in concentration as he gripped his friend's shoulder.

I glanced at Elias and found him staring at me, so I held his gaze unwaveringly. In the context of omegas and their alphas, that was actually a huge act of defiance, which showed just how fucked up this whole thing was. A few seconds later, a shiver passed through me, and I drew a sharp breath. I felt empty all of a sudden, and it was horrible and deeply jarring.

Carter let go of both of us and said, "Okay, I think it's done."

I whispered, "It is," and took a step backwards.

Elias looked as lost as I felt, which was a big change from his usual brash confidence. He walked to the edge of the field and stood with his back to us as Carter asked me, "Are you alright?" I nodded, and when the wind started to pick up, he said, "I'd better go before the storm hits." He took a business card from a thin, silver case and handed it to me. "Call me from the satellite phone if you need anything. I'll be back a week from today to restore the bond and take you wherever you want to go. In the meantime, I hope you two find some common ground."

I stuck the card in my pocket as I said, "Thank you, Carter." It was probably weird to thank someone who'd kidnapped me, but I liked him despite myself.

He gave my hand an affectionate squeeze as he said, "Good luck."

I retreated to the back of the house while he returned to the helicopter. The blades began to spin, whipping the dead grass, and soon it rose into the pale gray sky. I raised a hand to wave goodbye, then watched until it was out of sight.

Elias was about ten yards away, and he turned to me with a look of determination. I squared my shoulders and waited to see which of us would make the first move.

Chapter 4

Elias and I watched each other for a long moment. Then he seemed to make up his mind about something and strode across the field.

He came to a stop just inches from me, and we studied each other closely. I'd wondered if he'd still seem as handsome without the influence of our mate bond, and the answer was a huge, resounding yes. In fact, he was the most beautiful man I'd ever seen. His scent was wonderfully appealing too, even if he wasn't registering as my mate.

I figured he'd probably yell at me, but instead he did the last thing I would have predicted—he pulled me to him and kissed me. It was hungry and passionate, and I sank into it, clutching the front of his wool overcoat with both hands as my cock swelled. I'd expected to mean absolutely nothing to him without the bond, so it was another surprise when he whispered, "God, I missed you."

He liked the fact that I was getting turned on, and he nuzzled the side of my neck as he breathed in my scent. I yelped in surprise when he picked me up and tossed me over his shoulder, and as he carried me to the house I blurted, "What are you doing?"

"Taking you to bed."

I couldn't even pretend it didn't totally turn me on. He could smell it on me anyway, so even if I tried to claim I didn't want this, he'd know I was lying.

Elias finally put me down when we reached a sitting room on the second floor. He pushed my ski jacket off my shoulders, and it dropped to the floor as his hands slid down my arms. I really hadn't expected this much mutual attraction without the bond, but he was as aroused as I was. I hadn't even expected him to like me. Then again, he could probably hate me and want to fuck me at the same time.

When he licked the side of my neck, a tremor went through me. My cock strained against my jeans, but I made a feeble attempt at slowing this down as I murmured, "There's a lot I need to say to you." Instead of replying, he claimed my mouth in another rough kiss, which short-circuited my brain and transferred all the decision-making to my cock.

Even if our so-called relationship was one huge disaster, on this level we were perfectly in tune. And what an opportunity! I never thought I'd get a chance at what was basically a free pass. The first time a mated pair had sex usually held all kinds of significance and sealed their bond. This time though, we could just enjoy each other without a million complications.

Okay, so this probably wouldn't end up being totally complication-free, but I needed it desperately. I was starved for touch, for sex, for affection. For Elias. I grabbed him in an embrace and deepened his kiss as he caressed my body.

There was no way he was going to make this easy on me, not after I ran away and hid from him, so it didn't surprise me when he said, "You need to be punished for ignoring our bond and making me live without my mate for a century." He cupped my ass and gave it a squeeze as he whispered in my ear, "I'm going to wait for you in the bedroom. Take off all your clothes and come join me."

A soft moan escaped me when he bit my earlobe, and I asked, "What are you going to do to me?"

"I'm going to spank you, and then I'm going to fuck you so long and so hard that you forget your own name. You have to come to me naked, though. That's nonnegotiable." He held the back of my neck as he kissed me again, and desire burned through me.

When he let go of me and went into the other room, I instantly missed his scent, his touch, all of him. I adjusted my hard cock and took a breath. There'd really been no point in suppressing the mate bond. Lust had just taken its place and obliterated all my higher brain functions anyway.

Even if this was a terrible idea, I wanted it desperately. All of it, including the spanking, which turned me on in ways I couldn't explain and never anticipated. So, was I really going to do this? I'd hated him when we met, or I'd tried to tell myself I did. I hadn't wanted a mate, so maybe I'd latched on to every possible reason to reject him.

But despite everything, he was a part of me. That became crystal clear the moment the bond was muted and I felt his absence. In all that time, all those years, I'd never been able to shake one inescapable fact—we belonged to each other. It was why I'd never been able to sleep with anyone else. I swore under my breath and started unbuttoning my shirt.

Once I was naked, I hurried to the bedroom before I had a chance to talk myself out of it. Elias was sitting on the edge of a large, four-poster bed that was made up with dark red linens. He'd taken off his coat and rolled back the sleeves of his black dress shirt, but he was still fully clothed. I hesitated in the doorway with my hands covering my cock, breathing quickly as my heart pounded.

If he'd been cruel and demanding right then, I would have turned and ran. But instead, he held his hand out to me and said, "Come here, *mi amor*."

I rushed across the room, climbed onto his lap, and hid my face in the spot where his neck met his shoulder. He held me and caressed me while I breathed him in and tried to relax.

There was no reason to be scared. I was the one in control, no matter what it looked like. I was choosing this, and I chose to obey when he told me, "Lay across my lap, so I can spank you."

This really wasn't the time to try to analyze why I wanted this so much, or why it made my cock so hard that it ached. Instead, I did as he asked, positioning myself with my hard-on pressed against his thigh. I folded my arms on the bed and tucked my face into them, and then I held my breath.

I made a point of keeping quiet as he brought his hand down on my ass. As he did it again and again, I exhaled slowly and relaxed into it. This whole situation could have been humiliating. It could have been a lot of things, and it certainly stung a bit. But it was also deeply erotic, and I was glad it went on for a while.

Eventually, he took a small, round tub from the nightstand, which contained something like shea butter—not lube, strictly speaking, but it would do the job. He scooped up some of the thick cream, then worked a finger into my ass while I moaned softly.

He went back to lightly spanking me while he worked on opening me up. My ass cheeks were sore by that point, so even without any force behind them, each slap reverberated through me. I never asked him to stop. I didn't want him to.

When he started massaging my prostate, everything intensified. I squirmed on his lap, desperate for some friction against my throbbing cock. Meanwhile, he worked a second finger into me. I was wild with need by that point, and I tried to push myself onto his fingers as I begged him to fuck me.

Finally, he slipped his fingers from my ass and wiped his hands on a cloth he'd produced out of nowhere, then turned me over in his arms as he stood up. He placed me on the bed, positioning me on my side. I understood why when sitting up made my spanked ass ache.

As I waited impatiently for him to strip, it occurred to me how lucky it was that people with werewolf blood were immune to human diseases. It wasn't like either of us planned for this and brought condoms, and thankfully we didn't need them.

Once he was naked, he climbed onto the bed, pulled me to him, and kissed me like he needed it to live. I ran my fingers into his hair and got lost in that kiss, parting my lips, tasting his mouth while my hands slid over his big, powerful body.

I couldn't wait another minute, so I rolled onto my knees and elbows, and he lubed his cock. He folded a pillow and stuck it underneath my hips to help hold me up, and he pushed my legs apart. I clutched the blanket and held my breath as his tip pressed against my hole.

Then I started to panic. Maybe it wouldn't fit, or maybe he'd force it. But he stroked my lower back with a surprisingly gentle touch and murmured, "You're okay, Mateo. Just try to relax. Let yourself open up for me."

I tried to do as he said, and he pushed again. After a moment, his cockhead slid into me. I whimpered, overwhelmed by the sudden feeling of fullness, the stretch, the discomfort, but he kept talking to me, quietly, soothingly. I took a deep, shaky breath, then another.

When he felt me open up a little, he slid into me slowly. As my ass stretched and the feeling of fullness intensified, I whimpered again. He leaned down and wrapped an arm around my shoulders as he told me, "You're doing great, Mateo, and I'm proud of you." It was exactly what I needed to hear.

When I relaxed again, he pushed forward. Once he bottomed out in me, he held still and let me get used to the feeling of being impaled on his thick cock. He was so patient, more than I'd ever expected. He rubbed my back and spoke to me reassuringly while I concentrated on breathing.

He began moving in me, slowly at first. It hurt—until it didn't. Okay, so maybe the pain never really went away, but I stopped caring when the tip of his cock grazed my prostate. Waves of pleasure rolled through me, and he began taking me harder and harder until he was absolutely pounding my ass.

I reached up and grasped the top of the wooden headboard with both hands, bracing myself while he clutched my hips and drove himself into me. I became nothing but pure sensation, moaning and driving myself onto him, meeting each thrust. A moment before he came, he pulled me against him and bit my shoulder, which would have meant he claimed me as his mate if the bond had been in play.

I reached back, tangling my fingers in his hair as he came in me, his body slamming into mine so hard that he lifted me off my knees. He grasped my cock, and it only took a couple of strokes before I exploded, pushing into his hand and shooting across the blanket as a yell tore from me. It was intense and wild and by the time it ended, I was absolutely shattered.

I tried to curl into myself as he eased his cock from me. He gathered me up, holding me against his chest while he tossed aside the top blanket and wrapped us in the one underneath. All I could do was cling to him as we both caught our breath.

After a while, he whispered, "You were a virgin." I nodded. "I can't believe you actually waited for me."

"That wasn't the plan. I was so angry after we spent those three days together, and I really didn't think we'd ever end up here. I tried to sleep with other men, but somehow I could never go through with it. They just weren't…you."

"You really surprised me today."

"You surprised me, too." I ran my fingers over his collarbone, and after a moment I said, "Thanks for being careful with me when you realized it was my first time."

He shifted a bit and settled in. "I'll always take care of you, Mateo. That's my job as your alpha, just like it's your job to obey me."

That felt like a splash of cold water in the face. I whispered, "Damn it, Elias. Why did you have to say that?"

"Because it's true."

I sat up and turned to look at him. "You get that this was exactly the problem last time, right? You kept treating me like a possession instead of a person, and I didn't want any part of that."

"The problem last time was that you were stubborn and willful, and you refused to listen."

I took a deep breath and tried to remain calm. "I'll gladly submit to you when we're having sex. You can be totally in charge and I'll do whatever you say, because it turns out I actually like that. But outside the bedroom, I need you to treat me as an equal. That's not optional."

He sat up too, with some kind of strong emotion glinting in his dark eyes. "Look where we are right now, Mateo. Do you think I wanted to spend the last three months hiding out on this godforsaken island? The reason I'm here is because I have some very powerful enemies, and if they come for me and I tell you to run and hide, I need you to do as I say. How can I keep you safe if I can't trust you to obey me?"

"I don't need you to keep me safe, and I sure as hell wouldn't run and hide if we were in danger! I'm a grown man with enough warlock in me to be able to protect both of us against whatever comes our way."

His voice rose as he exclaimed, "That arrogance could get you killed! You think you're invincible, but you're just not."

"Look who's talking about being arrogant!" I climbed out of bed and told him, "Also, I don't buy this new angle of yours that it's all about keeping me safe. You've always wanted an obedient little pet, not a partner."

"You don't know what I want," he growled. "You didn't stick around long enough to find out."

"You made it pretty fucking clear in a short amount of time."

I started to leave the bedroom with the blanket wrapped around me like a toga, and he asked, "Where are you going?"

"Anywhere but here, before we both say things we'll regret."

I cut through the adjoining room and scooped up my clothes and shoes, then went downstairs and looked around me. God, what a creepy place. It was all dark wood paneling, antique furnishings, and heavy tapestries, like someone had deliberately tried to make it look haunted.

After quickly exploring the ground floor, I retreated to a library at the back of the building. Compared to the rest of the place, this room was a bit brighter, with two large windows overlooking the field behind the house. But only a bit, because it was overcast outside and pouring rain, and that gloom seemed to permeate everything.

I got dressed, then curled up in a wingback chair with the blanket and sighed. For a few minutes there, I'd started to feel opti-mistic, like maybe we actually had a chance of making this work. Or maybe we were doomed to repeat the same arguments, locked in an endless cycle of seeing who could be more stubborn.

Chapter 5

Maybe an hour later, I heard a faint rustle out in the hall. Then the door creaked slightly, and I realized Elias had taken a seat on the floor and was leaning against it.

I'd been staring out the window, and I set aside the book I'd forgotten about, crossed the room, and put my hand on the door. I wished I could read his mind. It was easy with some people, but werewolves' thoughts tended to be a chaotic, nonverbal jumble. A minute ticked by, and when nothing happened, I asked, "Why are you sitting out there?"

"I wanted to be close to you, but I figured you needed some time to yourself."

That was actually really touching. It was also totally unlike the Elias I thought I knew, because when we first met, he absolutely would have barged in uninvited and tried to order me back upstairs.

I sat down too and leaned against the door, so we were back-to-back. "Why did you want to be close to me?"

"Without our bond, it feels like a part of me is missing. That feeling goes away when we're together."

I admitted, "I feel the same way."

"Explain to me again what Carter's little magic trick was trying to accomplish."

"It was supposed to let us deal with each other as two rational, clear-headed people, as opposed to pheromone-crazed mates. When I'm under our bond's influence, all I want to do is fuck and submit to you."

"So, you do realize the very first thing you did without the bond was fuck and submit to me," he said.

"I know. It's very confusing." I sighed and fidgeted with the hem of my shirt.

"What exactly do you think I would do if you fully surrendered to me?"

"I don't want to find out," I said, as I wrapped my arms around myself. "The only person I can rely on is me. That's how it's always been, and that's how I want it."

His voice was gentle when he asked, "What happened to make you think you can't rely on anyone?"

I fought back a wave of emotions as I muttered, "I don't want to talk about it."

He fell silent for a minute before asking, "Are you hungry?"

"Yeah, I am." I was glad he changed the subject.

"Join me in the kitchen if you want to. If not, I'll leave a tray outside your door in a few minutes."

The door swayed, just a little, and there was a faint rustling sound. Then he was gone.

I stretched my legs out in front of me and exhaled slowly as I replayed our conversation. I liked the change in him. He seemed kinder, and he was actually talking to me instead of just ordering me around. But was he showing me the real Elias, or just what he thought I wanted to see? I wasn't sure people ever really changed—not to that degree, anyway—and I wondered how much of this I should believe.

After a while, I got to my feet and left the library, then found my way to the kitchen. I still didn't know what to think of his miraculous transformation, but he was making an effort, so I was going to do the same.

The kitchen turned out to be plainer and simpler than the rest of the house, functional instead of ornate. This house had obviously been built for people who had a staff to do the cooking.

Elias was pulling a loaf of bread out of the oven when I arrived, with a pair of big, red mitts on his hands. It was odd to see him doing something so domestic. He'd always struck me as a lord of the manor type, someone used to giving orders and having others do his bidding, just like whoever had built this house.

I asked, "Who owns this place?"

"I do."

"Why do you own a haunted house off the coast of Maine?"

"Someone signed it over to me to settle a debt. I'd been planning to sell it, but then it seemed perfect when I needed to disappear for a while." He ditched the mitts, then turned to a large pot on the stove and added, "I wish it really was haunted, by the way. I could have used the company these past three months."

I lingered in the doorway and eyed the loaf of bread hungrily as I asked, "Did you actually bake that?"

"I did. Not now, obviously, since it takes hours to make bread. I just stuck it in the oven to warm it up. The soup was also made yesterday, but I think it's much better the next day."

"It's surprising to see you cooking."

"Admittedly, I hadn't done much of it in recent years. But I've had a lot of time to kill while I've been on the island," he said. "It's given me a chance to practice some of the skills I learned when I lived in Provence."

"When was that?"

"Ages ago. I left Spain when I was thirty, then spent a few years in London before relocating to the south of France for the better part of four decades. I missed the food once I moved to the U.S., so I learned to make it myself."

He stirred the soup pot while I leaned against the doorframe and watched him. Elias was the type of man who somehow just belonged in a suit. But here he was, looking sexy and approachable in a pair of jeans, with the sleeves of his black Henley pushed back.

It was tough to reconcile this version of him with the one I thought I knew, but I liked him like this. He was much less intimidating.

To make conversation, I asked, "Why did you leave Spain?"

A shadow passed over his features as he muttered, "After my parents died, there was no reason to stay."

I knew there had to be a tragic story behind that. Elias was roughly half-werewolf, half-human, so either one parent was a full-blooded werewolf, or both carried a high percentage of that DNA. Anyone who was at least a quarter werewolf should have lived for hundreds of years. Since they'd been of child-bearing age thirty years before, that suggested they'd died very young.

It was obviously a painful subject though, so I didn't ask. Instead, I took a seat at the scarred wooden table at the back of the kitchen, near a brick fireplace with a fire burning brightly in its hearth. After a minute, I said, "I think this is the only warm spot in the entire haunted mansion."

"Yeah, the radiators don't seem to do much, so my advice is to seek out rooms with fireplaces. There are nine of them throughout the house."

Elias put two steaming bowls of lobster bisque on the table, then brought a platter of sliced bread with butter and sat down across from me. He watched me closely as I tried a small spoonful of soup, and I murmured, "Oh my god."

He actually seemed anxious as he asked, "Is something wrong?"

"No, not at all. It's literally the best thing I've ever eaten."

He looked relieved as I went back for a bigger spoonful. "I've never cooked for anyone before," he said. "I had no idea if what I liked would actually appeal to you."

"This is shockingly delicious. Seriously, how is it this good?"

"It's probably the fresh lobster. That's one of the nice things about being in Maine."

"You're being modest. You're great at this, and you can cook for me anytime," I said, between mouthfuls of that rich, savory soup.

"If you stay with me, I'll gladly cook for you every day."

I didn't really know what to say to that, so I ended up mumbling something along the lines of, "You wouldn't have to do that. It's not your job to feed me."

"It's my job as your alpha to take care of you, and this falls under that heading."

"I'm pretty sure that was never meant to include cooking. As the bigger and stronger of the pair, it's an alpha's job to defend their helpless little mate against outside threats." I infused as much sarcasm as I could into the helpless bit.

"It's the twenty-first century," he said, as a lopsided grin curved the corner of his mouth. "I can vanquish our foes and put dinner on the table if I want to. Don't hold me to your archaic standards."

I grinned, too. "And here I thought you were a total caveman. I mean, you are, in a lot of ways. But you're a caveman who likes to cook, so that's something."

"Finally! We've found one thing you like about me." There was a sparkle of amusement in his dark eyes. It was a good look on him.

"Actually, we've found two things in one day."

"What's the other thing?"

"You're phenomenal in bed."

"You have nothing to compare it to."

"No," I said, "but phenomenal is phenomenal."

"This is all great news. I'll see if I can manage a third thing before you take off for another hundred years."

After an awkward pause, I murmured, "I'm sorry I did that."

"Are you?"

"I wasn't sorry at the time, but I am now," I said.

"Because you realize you could have been eating this bisque all along?"

I chuckled at that, and his grin got a little wider. "Yes. That's obviously exactly what I meant."

I finished the soup, then used a piece of French bread to mop up the bottom of the bowl. He asked, "Would you like seconds?"

"Yes, please." That made him happier than it probably should have. He got up and refilled my bowl, then returned to his seat and tried to pretend he wasn't watching me eat, while he totally watched me eat.

After a while, he said, "I still can't believe you're here. I also couldn't believe it when Carter told me where he found you. Had you been living in the Hollywood Hills a long time?"

"Yeah, for about a quarter-century."

He shook his head in disbelief. "I was only about twenty miles away for the last two decades. I know L.A. is huge, and we only sense each other's presence if we're less than half a mile away. But still, it seems like we would have occasionally crossed paths, more than just that one time three months ago when I was on my way to the airport."

"I made sure that wouldn't happen by going into hiding."

He asked, "Do you mean you stayed in the house?"

"No. I spent twenty-four years as a warlock's familiar while disguised in animal form. I actually just shifted back last fall, after Griffin's full powers came in and he didn't really need me looking out for him anymore." I grinned and added, "It took several days to get used to walking on two legs again."

Elias looked shocked. "You can do that? It should be impossible for anyone but a pure werewolf to shift into his wolf form."

"Oh, it is. I had help transforming and turning back, from people with far more magical ability than I'll ever have. Also, I didn't disguise myself as a wolf. That would have attracted too much attention in L.A."

"Then what form did you take? Please don't tell me it was a black cat." He looked like he was ready to be offended on behalf of our canine counterparts, which I thought was pretty funny.

"No, it was a dog."

"Well, that makes sense," he said. "A husky or malamute would be really close to a wolf."

"Yeah, it wasn't either of those."

"Was it a German shepherd? And I actually envy you, as odd as that may sound."

"Why?"

"Every part werewolf I've ever met has this intense longing to be able to shift into our animal form. You were actually able to experience it for a while."

I glanced at him, then looked away as I said, "It wasn't a German shepherd, either," before scooping some more soup into my mouth.

"Then what form did you take?"

"Okay, so, what you have to realize is that I chose to become a familiar when the warlock was just a baby. After Griffin's parents were killed, he and I went to live with an older woman, a friend of the family who didn't know things like warlocks and werewolves existed. I couldn't exactly be something big and ferocious."

His grin turned teasing. "I can't wait to hear this."

I frowned at him before admitting, "I was an English bulldog."

Elias burst out laughing. I'd actually never seen him do that before. It was a great laugh, too—loud, uninhibited, and totally undignified, and it made me chuckle. When he could finally speak again, he said, "Please tell me there are pictures."

"Sure, lots of them. I'd show you some that Griffin sent me, but my phone was left behind when your demon abducted me."

"Yeah, sorry about that."

I ate some more bisque before saying, "I forgot to ask Carter how he knew he'd found me when he traced the fireworks to my house. He started knocking down my wards before he ever laid eyes on me."

"I let him read my mind, and he memorized your scent. I'm sure he detected it as soon as he arrived at your home."

"That explains it."

"For the record, I would have preferred to come to you myself, but I really can't set foot in L.A. right now."

I teased, "Well, I guess I can forgive you for not abducting me personally."

"At least Carter's polite, and he probably orchestrated a very well-mannered abduction."

"He did, apart from the bit where he went after my wards with the psychic equivalent of a battering ram and scared the shit out of me." I finished my soup before asking, "Who are you hiding from? Because whoever they are, I'm pretty sure your astonishingly powerful demon friend could kick their ass."

"Normally, you'd be right. There's almost nothing as powerful as Carter, with two exceptions."

I stared at him and said, "Carter told me there are a total of three demons on earth. Please don't tell me you befriended one and made enemies of the other two."

"Unfortunately, that's it exactly."

I put down my spoon and exhaled slowly as that sunk in. Then I muttered, "That's bad, Elias. Really, really bad. The darkness and power I sensed in Carter was terrifying, and if they're the same—"

"They are, and that's why I've put a continent between us."

"What if they find you? Will they kill you?"

"Not right away. That'd be too merciful," he said. "Centuries of torture is more their style."

"So, what are we going to do about this?"

"We're going to avoid getting caught. Carter warded the hell out of this island, and he also conjured a series of perimeter alarms that surround us like domes, so we'll know if anything's coming."

"But what if they break through? How can we possibly defend ourselves against a pair of demons?"

"We don't have to defend ourselves," he said. "We just have to get away, and they probably wouldn't come for me themselves. That sort of thing seems like it's beneath them. It's more likely they'd send their foot soldiers, and by the time they figured out how to get around the wards, we'd be long gone."

"Foot soldiers suggests they have an army."

I grimaced when he said, "Just a small one." After a pause, he added, "I'm sorry for dragging you into the middle of this, although I think you're much safer here than in L.A. You were practically right in their backyard, and if they'd ever linked you to me, they wouldn't have hesitated to use you as leverage."

I asked, "What did you do to get on their bad side?"

"I got close to them and earned their trust, and then I took down their human trafficking operation from the inside. I think you know most of the ways I make a living are illegal, so it was easy enough to get an introduction and ingratiate myself to them. They never saw it coming."

"You did that on your own?" When he nodded, I asked, "Why wouldn't you go to the police, or the FBI?"

"What could human law enforcement possibly do to two powerful demons?"

He had a point. "What happened to the victims?"

"I freed seventy-two people from a holding facility and got them all to safety. I also managed to turn the traffickers' entire network against each other before I was found out. It'll take them a while to rebuild, if they even bother. Demons get bored easily, so they might have found a new way to entertain themselves at humankind's expense by now."

I reached across the table and took his hand as I said, "What you did was really brave, and I'm proud of you."

"It was just a drop in the bucket," he muttered. "I wish I could have driven them out once and for all, but I'm totally powerless against them. I hate that feeling."

"It was more than a drop in the bucket to the people you saved."

He squeezed my hand, then let go of it and got up. As he started to clear the table, he said, "That's my only consolation, but all I can think about is how many more people the brothers could hurt on a whim, and the fact that no one on earth has enough power to stop them."

"The brothers?"

"That's what people call the demons, because they're inseparable. Their real names are unpronounceable, so they've taken to calling themselves Cain and Abel. Don't ask me why. It always seemed like an odd choice."

We both fell silent as we turned our attention to cleaning up the kitchen. When we finished, Elias asked, "Would you like to go for a walk? It actually stopped raining, but that might not be the case for long."

"Sure. Let me grab my coat."

We met at the front door a few minutes later. Elias had added boots, a black peacoat, and a black wool scarf to his ensemble, and he looked polished and pulled together. Meanwhile, I looked like a kid who was about to go sledding in my puffy, cream-colored ski jacket. In my defense, I hadn't exactly planned ahead for any of this. I also hadn't had a chance to pack a bag, so my jeans and light blue button-down would have to be my uniform for the foreseeable future.

As we cut across the field at the back of the house, Elias asked, "Have you forgiven me for whatever I said earlier to make you angry?"

"It's the same thing you always say, which basically comes down to omegas being obedient little lap dogs."

"I never said—" Elias cut himself off, then pushed his hair back from his eyes. "Never mind."

He took my hand as we cut through the trees on a well-worn path. After a minute, we emerged at a rocky overlook, and I said, "This is really beautiful." Half a dozen islets dotted the rough, gray sea, each its own miniature world of rocks and trees.

"It is. I'm trying to appreciate it, instead of resenting the fact that I've been stuck here with the same view for ninety-three days." When I shivered a little, he said, "Come here." Then he unbuttoned his coat and held out his arms.

I slipped my hands inside his coat and around his waist, then leaned into him. His warmth and scent surrounded me, and it was wonderfully soothing.

He wrapped his arms around me and rested his cheek against my hair. After a few moments I asked, "How can you be so different now than when we first met? You don't even seem like the same person."

"A century is a long time. People change."

"Do they, though?"

"Sure," he said, "when they have sufficient motivation."

"What was your motivation?"

"You. I was determined not to drive you away when I found you again, like I did the first time."

"That wasn't all you. I probably overreacted."

"No, you didn't. I was horrible to you when we met. I won't make excuses for my behavior, but I want you to know I'm sorry."

I murmured, "Go ahead and make excuses. Tell me what was going on with you."

"I don't think you're going to like this story."

"Tell me anyway." I nestled against his chest and listened to his heartbeat.

"Well, alright." After a pause, he said, "As you know, the majority of part werewolves don't have fated mates. I'd gone eighty years without one and figured it wasn't in the cards for me, so I ended up falling in love with a human. We wanted to build a life together, but then he was killed."

"Oh god, Elias, I'm so sorry."

Several seconds passed before he continued, "Four months later, I met you and our mate bond engaged. I felt so many things when that happened, including anger and confusion, all jumbled together with that overwhelming pull to be with you. I felt like I was betraying Jannik's memory, even though I know you and I didn't have any say in what was happening to us."

I said softly, "You should have told me about him."

"I thought you'd be furious that your mate tried to couple with someone else."

"But it was before we met."

"I know, but it's not like our emotions under the bond's influence are rational. Just the opposite, they're intense and all-consuming, bordering on obsession."

"You're right," I said. "But I like to think I would have understood."

"There's more." He took a breath and said, "His death was my fault. I got in a fight with one of my shady business partners, and the man pulled a gun on me. Jannik got in the way of the bullet and died trying to save me. I begged him not to come to my office that night. I told him it was dangerous, but he wouldn't listen. He never listened, and it got him killed."

I said softly, "No wonder you were so adamant about my obedience."

"You're a lot like him—willful and stubborn, sweet and beautiful. I can't lose you too, Mateo. I won't survive it."

"I'm not sweet."

"Sure you are."

After a pause, I asked, "Do I look like him, too?"

"He was a tall, forty-year-old, blue-eyed blond from Denmark, so no. Not even a little. Why do you ask?"

"I don't know. I guess…I guess I just wondered if I was the universe's idea of a consolation prize or something, after you lost your one true love."

"That's not how it works," he said. "Even though the mate bond doesn't engage until the younger of the pair turns twenty, it's a part of us from the day we're born, and—"

"I know, and I've always had a hard time with the idea that I was made for you. Like, the reason I'm gay is because you are, since I was literally born to be your mate."

"Actually, we were made for each other," he said. "I was born with the bond, too."

"I never thought about it like that." I tilted my head back to look up at him and grinned. "You know, that means you belong to me, every bit as much as I belong to you."

"Of course I do."

"In that case, do I get to tell you what to do?"

He smiled at me. "Your wish is my command. What would you like me to do?"

"Nothing right now, but I'm sure I'll think of something."

"Keep me posted." He sounded amused.

After a while, we started walking again. It was definitely cold, but I liked the fresh sea air and the sound of the waves crashing on the rocks below. The best part, though, was the feeling of Elias's hand in mine. It was warm and comforting, and it made me feel secure for some reason.

As we followed the curve of the island on a trail above the rocky shore, I asked, "What happens when this week is up, Elias? The mate bond will kick in, I know that. It turns out we're drawn to each other no matter what, so I guess it won't make a huge difference. What'll we do, though? Do we keep living on this island until you decide it isn't safe anymore?"

"I think we need to wait and see how you feel about everything at the end of the week, before we start making plans. I hope you'll want to stay with me, but that's up to you."

"If I wanted to leave, would you let me?"

He glanced at me and said, "I have no intention of holding you prisoner. I'd beg you not to return to L.A. though, because you really shouldn't be that close to the brothers."

"But how would they find me? It took you decades, and they don't even know I exist."

"Their abilities and resources are way beyond anything I ever had, and it wouldn't be difficult for them to find out I have a mate. I hired several people to search for you over the years, and I provided each of them with your name, all the details I knew about you, and a drawing of what you look like. Any one of them could potentially pass that information along to the brothers."

"Even if they did, nothing's under my name, including my house and car. I don't even have a credit card."

He grinned a little. "You were pretty serious about hiding from me."

"I made it a way of life."

"That's a testament to just how awful I was when we first met."

"But I understand what you were going through, and I also know I played a big part in what went wrong between us. I was angry and resentful, and I never really gave you a chance," I said. "The thing is, I'd just emigrated to the U.S. with all these hopes and plans. My first nineteen years were hell, and I thought I was finally going to get a chance to build the life I'd always wanted. Then I turned twenty, and you showed up out of nowhere and tried to take over. It seemed like my independence and everything I'd been working for was going to be taken from me, along with my free will."

"I can see why you had such a hard time with our bond," he said.

"Even so, I feel incredibly guilty about running away, and all the years I spent hiding."

It started to rain, so Elias led me to a covered bench on the hillside above the boathouse, and we sat down side-by-side. Then he said, "We were both struggling when we met, and the bond caught us totally off guard. We lived with the consequences of those three disastrous days for a long time, and now we have a chance to get it right." He turned to meet my gaze as he continued, "But to do that, we have to shift our focus to the present, instead of dwelling in the past."

"You're right." He leaned in and kissed me, and after a moment, I murmured, "Damn it, Elias."

"What's wrong?"

"Nothing. It's just that you're amazing, and I can't believe I wasted an entire century hiding from you. We lost so much time because of me, and—"

He interrupted with, "Remember what we just said? We're done looking back."

I nodded and climbed onto his lap. He wrapped his arms around me and kissed me again, and it was sweet and tender. I parted my lips and deepened the kiss, tasting him and offering myself at the same time.

All around us, the wind howled and the rain came down in sheets. But here in our own little world on that bench, I felt safe, and warm, and protected.

Chapter 6

Elias and I spent quite a while on that bench, wrapped up in each other and deep in conversation as the rain came down. When we finally decided to move indoors, we joined hands and ran to the house, getting soaked along the way.

We hung our wet coats in the foyer, and he picked me up and carried me upstairs. The stubborn part of me wanted to argue that I was capable of walking on my own, but the rest of me shouted at that part to shut the hell up and enjoy it.

Elias drew a bath, and while the big, claw-footed tub filled with hot water, he worked on building a fire in the brick fireplace in the bedroom. After his third match failed to light, I flicked my fingers and the logs went up in flames. He glanced at me with a grin and said, "I almost had it."

"I know. Just thought I'd help."

He straightened up and brushed his hands against each other as he said, "It's easy to forget you have those abilities. You don't use them very often."

"I'm used to keeping them hidden, same as everyone with enough witch or warlock blood to work a spell. It's never been safe to risk revealing ourselves to humans, so hiding becomes second-nature, even when we really don't have to."

"I've always been curious," he said, as he came up to me and started unbuttoning my shirt. "Just how powerful are you?"

I shrugged. "I could pick up that big, four-poster bed with a thought, but I couldn't knock down this building. I guess that means on the scale of party tricks to real power, I'm pretty far down at the party trick side. But I do have the ability to read minds, which might nudge me slightly toward the power end of the spectrum."

He stopped unbuttoning the shirt. "You're kidding." I shook my head, and he said, "That's incredibly rare."

"I know. It's probably a result of the way my warlock and werewolf sides combined in me. Often when two different paranormal species come together, the result is something brand new."

"This is both fascinating and embarrassing. What sorts of ridiculous things have I been thinking while we've been together?"

"I can't really read you. Like most werewolves, it comes across as a nonverbal, chaotic jumble, and almost never just a clear thought."

He grinned and muttered, "Well, thank god for that."

I grinned, too. "If I'd been able to read your thoughts, what would I have discovered?"

"That I'm horribly sappy and not nearly as invulnerable as I like to pretend I am."

He went back to unbuttoning my shirt, and when he pulled it off me, I said, "So, we're getting naked now? Is that the plan?"

"Your jeans are soaked and you're shivering, so I'm planning to warm you up. Any objections?"

"None whatsoever."

"Good."

We hung my wet clothes on a chair in front of the fire, and he took my hand and led me to the adjoining bathroom. After he turned off the water, he gestured at the tub and said, "Hop in."

"Will you be joining me?"

"Actually, I'm going to bathe you."

I climbed into the tub and told him, "Just so you know, I'm really not used to stuff like this. You may want to pace yourself."

All he said to that was, "It's time you learn to be cared for."

Elias did exactly what he said he was going to, after first stripping down to just a pair of black briefs. He sat on the edge of the tub and washed me gently with a soft cloth and a bar of soap that smelled faintly of lemons. Then he shampooed and rinsed my hair. Meanwhile, I did something I usually found next to impossible—I relaxed and surrendered control.

I'd never expected us to be so comfortable around each other. I could only assume that familiarity was the result of sharing a bond for a century. But whatever the reason, it was pretty wonderful.

When the water started to cool, Elias pulled the plug, then held up a big towel for me. When I stepped into it, he wrapped his arms around me and dried me off before taking my hand and leading me to the bed.

The fire had warmed the room enough for us to stretch out on top of the covers. I trailed my fingers across his collar bone, then down his arm as I murmured, "There's so much I don't know about you."

"Ask me anything."

He stretched out on his side and propped his head up with his hand, and I met his gaze as I asked, "How are you making a living these days?"

His smile crinkled the corners of his eyes. "Are you asking if I'm still a criminal? That was a real sticking point with you last time."

"Yes. That's what I'm asking."

"I'm a nearly two-hundred-year-old part werewolf. What am I going to do, get a job in corporate America, then pretend to retire when they think I'm sixty-five, all while never appearing to age a day?"

"Well, no. But there are plenty of ways to earn money that aren't illegal."

"I've never been a part of mainstream society, so why should I obey their laws? In case you're concerned though, the ways I choose to make a living don't hurt anyone."

I rolled onto my side facing him, with one leg crossed over my junk, because I did have a shred of modesty. "There's no such thing as a victimless crime," I said.

"Well, okay, there are victims. I steal from the obscenely rich. But they certainly don't suffer for it, and I don't feel remotely guilty."

"So, you're basically Robin Hood."

"Hardly. I do make generous, anonymous donations to charity, but I've also kept plenty for myself. If you stay with me, you'll never want for anything. I made sure of it."

I gestured around us and asked, "Do you also do a bit of loan-sharking?"

"This island wasn't given to me to pay off a loan, it was to settle a poker debt. It used to belong to a sleazy tech billionaire, who bought it on a whim. Cocky bastard thought he could bluff while I was staring him down with a royal flush. And no, I didn't cheat to win, in case you're wondering. I didn't have to." He held my gaze as he asked, "Do you hate the fact that I occasionally break the law?"

"I probably should, but no, not really. I guess my moral compass is broken."

"Or maybe you've just been alive long enough by now to realize the world and its rules aren't black and white."

"Maybe."

He asked, "What about you? What do you do for a living?"

"I restore classic cars."

"Nice. How'd you get into that line of work?"

"I've always been a gearhead. I started building hotrods and street racing in the 1960s and 70s. Now I'm restoring those same makes and models, but they're insanely expensive collector items."

"I would have loved to see you race," he said, as he ran his hand down my thigh.

"It was a lot of fun, but I had to give it up after a while. Even though I moved around a lot, I was establishing a reputation in the street racing community and attracting attention. People start asking questions when you still look like you're twenty, but you've been racing for two decades."

"It's a shame you had to give it up."

"Honestly, I would have outgrown it anyway. I was reckless when I was younger. Now I'm content to be a homebody."

"You don't miss the excitement?"

I considered that before admitting, "Sometimes. It was definitely a rush."

"I can imagine." He grinned at me and said, "You might not love the fact that I'm a criminal, but you know, street racing isn't exactly legal."

"No, it's not. You're right that our kind don't fit into mainstream society. Maybe we're destined to…" My voice trailed off as his fingertips skimmed my butt, making my cock twitch.

He asked, "Are you still sore from earlier?"

"No. You know how fast werewolves heal."

His grin turned wicked. "That's good news."

A heated kiss soon turned into a wild afternoon of passion. We explored each other with our hands and tongues and lips, experimenting to see what brought the most pleasure. Once we were totally worked up, Elias pinned my hands to the mattress and fucked me, his body slamming into mine as I wrapped my legs around him. He was wild and uninhibited and so sexy, and when he growled, "You're mine," I moaned with pleasure.

"Say it," he said. "Let me hear the words."

I didn't even hesitate. "I'm yours." Saying it out loud was a rush. It was also the truth.

When he came in me, every thrust felt like he was staking a claim. And once he finished, he settled between my thighs and sucked my cock, edging me until I begged for release. When he finally let me come, I nearly blacked out as I yelled and writhed and shot down his throat.

Afterwards, we wrapped ourselves around each other, and I tried to catch my breath as my body shuddered with exhaustion. Surprisingly, I didn't fall asleep right away, but he did. I pulled the blanket up to his shoulders and watched him for a while.

This had been the most unexpected day imaginable, and Elias had proven to be the biggest surprise of all. I'd built him up to be a monster over the years, maybe to justify the fact that I'd left him, and to try to make myself feel less guilty. Sure, he'd been cold and domineering, but I should have given him some time. I'd made a huge mistake when I left, one that couldn't be changed, but I could do better moving forward.

We still had a lot to learn about each other, and there'd probably be some challenges down the road as we tried to fit our lives together. But I knew now, beyond a doubt, that I wanted this. I wanted *him*.

I'd been so afraid of all I'd lose if I gave in to our bond, including my freedom. But now I realized accepting my fate would bring me far more than I'd ever imagined.

The room was cold and dark when a loud noise pulled us both from a deep sleep a few hours later. I mumbled, "What was that?"

Elias sat up in bed, tense and alert, and told me, "That was Carter's perimeter alarm, the one set at sea level."

"Does that mean someone's coming for us?"

He turned on the light, and we both tumbled out of bed as he said, "I don't know for sure. A boat might randomly be headed directly toward the island, but who'd be out in this storm? Get dressed. We need to be ready to move, in case this isn't a false alarm."

We both pulled on our clothes as quickly as we could. Maybe a minute later, another sharp buzzing sound rang out. "That's the next perimeter alarm," he said. "They're moving fast, because those checkpoints are a mile apart."

My heart was racing as we dashed out of the bedroom and down the hall. He ducked into the study and grabbed the satellite phone off its changer. Then he took two things from a desk drawer. I couldn't tell what the smaller object was, but the other was a gun, which he stuck in the back of his waistband.

When we got downstairs, I threw on my coat, and we ran out the front door as a third alarm sounded. As we sprinted to the boathouse through the wind and pouring rain, I yelled, "How far from the island was that first perimeter checkpoint?"

"Five miles."

"At this rate they'll be here in two minutes!"

"They still have to get through Carter's wards, but I have a bad feeling about this."

I was relieved to discover the boathouse contained a high-end black speedboat with a long, pointy front end, which looked fast as hell. It was bobbing on the water in the center of the building, flanked by two bumper-lined walkways.

Elias punched a button just inside the door, and what was basically a garage door opener raised a gate at the far end of the building, opening it to the sea. I climbed into the boat, and he quickly untied the moorings, then jumped in beside me and dialed a number on the satellite phone.

When the call connected, Elias said, "Carter, it's me. Someone's coming. We're in the boat, in case we have to leave in a hurry." Another alarm sounded, and he added, "They're a mile out and moving unusually fast, especially in this storm."

My hearing was good enough to catch Carter's reply on the other end. "Sit tight," he said. "As long as you're behind the wards, you should be safe. I'm on my way, but it'll take time to get there."

"I doubt the helicopter can make it to the island. It's too windy."

"Then I'll steal a Coast Guard cutter, or whatever the hell can get me there. Is Mateo with you?"

"Yeah, he's right here." I closed my eyes and tried to reach out with my senses, and Elias asked me, "What are you doing?"

"Trying to see if I can get a read on whoever's coming, but they're too far away. When do the wards kick in?" Just then, the final alarm sounded as our soon-to-be visitor passed the one-mile mark.

Carter answered that one. Not surprisingly, his hearing was as good as mine. "The wards are set up two hundred yards from shore, and there's no way over or under them."

"As long as that's not the brothers themselves coming for us," I said.

"Yes. Well, let's hope they decided to send their lackeys on this errand," Carter said. "Assuming this even has anything to do with them. We don't know that yet."

"Why else would a boat be making a beeline for the island in this weather?" A few moments later, a tremor passed through me. I turned to Elias and asked, "Did you feel that?" He shook his head, and I told him, "They just sent out a wave of energy to test the wards."

He pushed his hair back from his forehead as he muttered, "Shit, so whoever it is has some magical ability."

Another wave of energy rolled over us, stronger this time, and a faint blue glow appeared out over the water for a moment. "I felt that one," Elias said. "What was that flash of light?"

"The wards just gave a little."

"That shouldn't be possible," Carter said. "Unless—"

Just then, I was able to locate whoever had come for us. I sensed darkness and unbelievable power, and I blurted, "It's a demon. I guess one of the brothers decided Elias was worth a house call."

Carter asked, "There's just one?"

"Yes, and there are three humans with him. Correction—three vampires." The sky lit up brighter blue as another shockwave rolled over us, and I said, "Our only chance is to make a break for it. The wards are collapsing. We probably only have a minute or two before they're totally dismantled."

"I'm going to run," he said, "but you need to stay here."

"What are you talking about?"

"I can lead him away from you. Then you'll be safe."

I exclaimed, "Absolutely not! I'm coming with you. That's not up for debate."

"But that could get you killed! Please, Mateo, I'm begging you. Stay here and hide. Carter has an additional set of wards on the boathouse. Unless the demon knocks them down, he can't sense you in here. Right now, he doesn't even know you exist."

"I'm not leaving your side, Elias. Not for any reason. I have magical ability and you don't, which means I can help!"

Elias dropped the phone and drew me into his arms. He kissed my forehead, and then he said, "Please don't be angry. This is for your own good."

He ran his thumb down the side of my throat, following the line of my jugular vein. There was something cold and wet on it. A wave of dizziness washed over me, and I stepped back and asked, "What did you do?"

He tossed aside a tiny glass vial, then picked me up just as my legs gave out and climbed out of the boat. "I used a potion Carter gave me to make you sleep for a while. I knew if we were discovered you wouldn't stay behind, not even if I begged you. This is the only thing that'll keep you safe. I'm going to hide you in the storage room. There's a final ward on it, so even if the boathouse wards are knocked out, no one will be able to see you or sense you're there."

"Hide with me." I tried to reach for him, but my arms felt so heavy.

"I can't." He cradled me against his chest as he carried me through the boathouse. "The only way this'll work is if I lure the demon away from you. Otherwise, he'll just tear down the rest of the wards and find us both. I'll make sure he sees me, and then I'll head for open water and try to outrun him. I'll also tell Carter where to find you, and he'll make sure you're okay."

"No! Don't go without me. I can help you." Everything was going out of focus, and I began slurring my words.

"You're no match for a demon. Neither am I, but at least I can do this—I can protect you, the only way I know how. You're everything to me, Mateo, and I hope you can forgive me."

I mumbled, "Please, Elias. Don't—"

In the next instant, everything went black.

Chapter 7

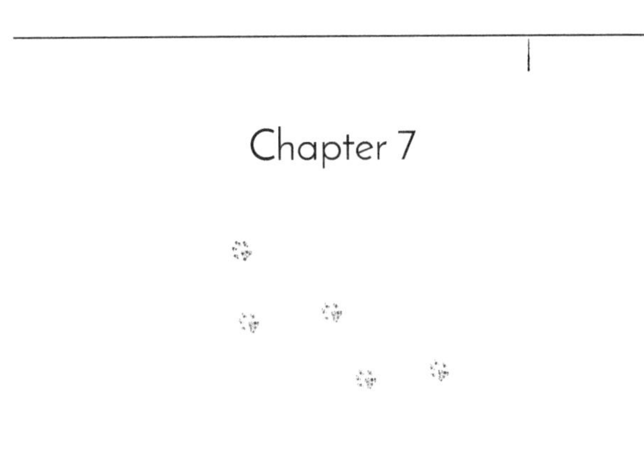

I awoke slowly. I was someplace cold and dark, and there was the sound of wind and water. My head ached, and my mouth was dry.

When I could, I sat up and looked around me. I was on a wood floor in a small room, covered by a wool blanket. It was hard to concentrate, and a few seconds ticked by before the fog lifted enough for me to remember what had happened.

I staggered to my feet, not quite free of the potion's effects, and opened the door to what turned out to be a small storage room. The boat was gone. I tried to reach out with my senses, but I couldn't find Elias.

As panic welled up in me, I rushed along the walkway, using the wall to steady myself. When I reached the open gate, I looked out over the choppy sea, but there was nothing but wind and rain and darkness.

I shivered and wrapped my arms around myself. I had no idea if Elias was safe, and I absolutely hated the fact that there was nothing I could do to help him.

Fear and anger fought for the top spot as I muttered, "Damn it, Elias." I knew he thought he was doing the right thing, but I didn't want to be left behind! I belonged at his side, so we could face whatever was happening together. Instead, he'd given me absolutely no choice in the matter, which was infuriating.

I retreated back a few feet to get out of the worst of the wind. Then I sat down on the walkway, pulled my hood up, and wrapped my arms around my knees.

There was no way of knowing how long I'd been unconscious. Not that it really made a difference. If it'd been five minutes or two hours, the result was the same. I was stuck here, helpless and frustrated, while somewhere in the night my mate might be fighting for his life.

Because it was the only thing I could do, I kept reaching out with my senses and trying to find Elias. Of course, that would only work if he was relatively close. Not like he'd come back here if he lost whichever of the brothers was pursuing him. It would be the first place the demon would look.

After a while, I felt a dark energy on the periphery of my senses. I could only hope it was Carter, but at this point I had no idea, so I got up and hurried back to the warded storage room. Then I looked around and picked up an old plank to use as a weapon, even though I knew that was ridiculous. If one of the brothers had come back for me, what was I going to do, smack him with it? All that'd do was get me killed faster.

As soon as the door was shut, I couldn't sense that dark energy anymore. Then I realized the concealment spell on the storage room was working both ways, blocking anything in or out. I hated feeling cut off like that.

Minutes ticked by. I felt nauseous and my anxiety was through the roof, but all I could do was wait.

Suddenly, the door to the storage room was flung open, and a tall, dark figure loomed before me. Instinctively, I threw the board at his head, then thrust my hand out and hit him right in the gut with a ball of pure energy.

Carter staggered back a few feet, stopping just short of falling in the water. Then he doubled over with his hands on his knees and muttered, "Ow."

I rushed to his side and asked, "Are you okay?"

He straightened up and dabbed at the spot on his forehead where the board had made contact. "I'm fine, but that didn't feel great."

"I couldn't tell who it was through the wards you put in place, and I was worried the other demon had doubled back."

"No, he's long gone. He got what he was looking for."

"He took Elias?" When he nodded, I asked, "Are you sure?"

"Elias's boat was drifting offshore with a disabled motor, so I dragged it onto the beach. There was no sign of him."

Anxiety coursed through me as I ran out of the boathouse. The rain had stopped, and the black speedboat was just a few yards away, listing to one side on the rocky shore. I used a ball of energy to light up the night and searched the boat's interior. There was no blood, no sign of a struggle, but the handgun was on the passenger seat. I threw it out into the water with a flick of my wrist. It wasn't going to stop a demon anyway, and I didn't want anyone stumbling across it.

Then I turned to Carter, who was folding up the collar of his black trench coat against the wind, and asked, "Can you restore my mate bond?"

"Now?" When I nodded, he said, "Alright," and grasped my wrist. He concentrated for a few moments, and I was overcome with relief when I felt the bond return. Carter let go of me and asked, "Did it work?"

"It did. I can feel it," I said, around the lump in my throat. "That means he's still alive. Thank god."

"We need to get back to L.A., since I assume that's where they're taking him. Come with me."

As we climbed the hill, I asked, "How long was I out?"

"Not long. Elias called me about an hour ago."

"I can't believe he knocked me out." We circled around to the back of the house, and I was surprised to see the helicopter on its concrete pad. "How did you fly here in these conditions?"

"It occurred to me that demons can actually do something about the weather—on a very small scale, at least."

I soon found out what he meant by that. Once we were seated in the helicopter with our headphones on, he positioned his hands palm-to-palm, then pulled them apart. I felt the change in air pressure in my inner ear, and all of a sudden the helicopter wasn't shaking from the wind anymore.

The rotors started up, and then we rose into the air in the little bubble of protection Carter had created around us. As we headed out over the water, I asked, "Would they really take him all the way back to L.A.?"

"I think so. If you only felt one of the brothers, my theory is that Cain sent Abel to fetch Elias. Cain's the more dominant of the two by far. He'll definitely want to be involved in whatever they do to him, but I doubt he could be bothered to fly cross-country to handle this in person."

"Are they going to kill him?"

"Eventually, but they'll torture him first." Carter frowned and added, "Let's just call that their specialty, as demons."

"How did they find him?"

"If I had to guess, I'd say they figured out a way to track me, and I led them directly to the island. I really thought I'd shielded myself enough to make that impossible, but I guess I underestimated what the two of them are capable of."

I kept up my barrage of questions with, "Do you know where to find the brothers, once we're back in L.A.?"

"Yes. They don't bother hiding, because they don't believe anyone's a threat to them. The real question is what we're going to do to get Elias back. There's nothing they want that we can trade for him, and we'll never outgun them. The two of them together aren't just twice as strong as I am. When they work together, they amplify each other's power exponentially."

I muttered, "Awesome." Then I fell silent, wrapping an arm around myself while I chewed the edge of my thumbnail.

After a while, Carter asked, "Aside from the part where he knocked you out, which I'm sure you're thrilled about, how was your time with Elias?"

"It was wonderful, up to that point."

"He was just—"

I cut him off with, "Don't tell me he was just trying to keep me safe, because I don't want to hear it. How could you give him that potion? How did it even come up? Did you phone him and say, 'hey, I captured your mate, and by the way do you want a way to render him unconscious?' Because that's just great, Carter."

"No! It was nothing like that."

"Explain it to me, then."

"Elias is the type of person to plan for every contingency," he said. "When I told him I was bringing you to the island, we discussed what might happen if the brothers ended up finding both of you there. He was sure you wouldn't cooperate and hide if he asked you to, and he was worried your stubbornness would get you killed. So, we came up with the idea of a mild sedative of sorts, only to be implemented as part of a worst-case scenario. We never really thought he'd need to use it, let alone on your first day together."

"Of all the things you could have given him." I shook my head. "Instead of worrying about how to incapacitate me, how about arming him with a fucking rocket launcher?"

"You can't kill a demon with conventional weapons."

"No, but you could slow him the hell down if you blow his boat out of the water."

"Point taken." After a pause, Carter muttered, "He was right, though."

"What do you mean?"

"I heard your conversation. There's no chance you would have stayed behind willingly tonight, and if you'd been on that boat when Abel swooped in, you'd either be dead now or you'd be their prisoner. Had they gone with the latter, they would have soon figured out hurting you did more harm to Elias than hurting him directly, and they would've had all kinds of fun torturing you."

"You don't know what would have happened," I said. "I might have been able to help."

"How?"

"Maybe I could have knocked out the engine on Abel's boat, before he took ours out. Or maybe I could have engulfed him in fog so he couldn't see where he was going, or capsized him, or—"

"That all sounds great," Carter interrupted, "but you'd have to get pretty close to the other boat to do any of that, because your magic's not very strong. Meanwhile, Abel could have snapped your neck with a flick of his finger, and Elias could have watched you die."

"Or maybe I could have protected him! I should have been allowed to try."

My voice broke, and Carter glanced at me and said, "You really care about him."

"Of course I do, and I need to save him."

"We will," he said.

"How?"

"We'll figure something out." That wasn't particularly reassuring.

Eventually, we arrived at the airport. It was almost deserted in that terrible weather, aside from Carter's pilot, who had the private jet all ready to go. We hurried across the tarmac and took a seat in the plane, and I said, "Before we take off, I need to use your phone."

As he handed it over, he asked, "Who are you calling?"

"My best friend. You and I are no match for the brothers, but if we add a powerful warlock to the mix, we might stand a better chance of surviving this."

When I dialed Griffin's number, it went straight to voicemail. I left a message that said, "This is Mateo, and I need your help, Griffin. I'm really sorry about interrupting your honeymoon, but this is an emergency. My mate's been taken prisoner by a pair of demons who are going to torture and kill him, and I don't think I can get him back without you. I don't have my phone, so please call me at this number when you get my message. I'll explain everything when I see you, but please come home, and hurry."

As I handed Carter's phone back to him, I said, "I don't know what else to do. Griffin and his husband Ari are currently in Paris, and it'll take time for them to make it back to California. Meanwhile, every minute Elias is in the brothers' hands is a minute too long."

"The brothers probably won't do anything to him until they're reunited, so I'll see if I can buy us a little time."

He started typing a message, and I asked, "What are you doing?"

"I'm sending some of my people to watch the airports for the brothers' private jet, and I'm asking others to stand by and be ready to disrupt Cain's little empire. If he's busy putting out fires, he won't have time to deal with Elias."

"That's a good idea," I said. "Are any of your people witches or warlocks?"

"Just one, my second-in-command, Desiree. Her powers aren't off the charts or anything, but she's smart and extremely capable. That's who I just messaged. Aside from her though, I tend to avoid people with magical ability."

"Why?"

He glanced at me, then looked away as he said, "Because they can sense the darkness in me, so I make them extremely uncomfortable. Somehow, it doesn't bother Desiree, but she's a rare exception."

"I could see how that might be a problem." After a few moments, I asked, "Does Elias have any witch or warlock friends who might be willing to help us?"

"No, he's a bit of a loner. What about you? Do you know anyone else with magical ability, besides the person you just called?"

"Griffin is friends with a couple of vampire-warlock hybrids. I don't know their number, but I'll ask him to contact them as soon as he calls me back. Then there's Griffin's husband, but I think Ari's pretty much out of gas."

"What does that mean?"

"He's a fallen angel. As I understand it, they only have a finite amount of magic when they fall, and once it's gone it's gone."

"That's really too bad. An angel at the height of their power would have definitely tipped the scales in our favor."

"Yeah, we're definitely not that lucky," I said, as the plane began taxiing toward the runway. "It's probably just going to be you, me, Desiree, and Griffin facing off against the big bad demon duo, assuming my friend even gets back to California in time. Maybe his vampire friends will back us up, maybe not. They barely know me, so I don't know why they'd put themselves in harm's way to help rescue my mate."

Carter muttered, "Those are truly awful odds."

Chapter 8

The cross-country flight seemed to take forever, though we actually made good time. My only consolation was the fact that the demon would have to travel the same distance to deliver my mate to his cohort. I had to cling to the hope that Elias was okay in the meantime.

A limo was waiting for us at LAX, and when we climbed into the back of it, Carter said, "Desiree Keene, say hello to Mateo Figueroa."

Desiree was a cute, curvy Black woman who looked like she was in her early twenties, but since she was part witch, there was every chance she was much older. She wore her hair in two puffy pigtails up high on her head, and she was dressed in a pink velour track suit and sneakers. "Black Girl Magic" was spelled out in rhinestones on her purple T-shirt, which was very literal in her case.

She looked up from her pink laptop. On the back of it was a sticker of Disney's Evil Queen, holding the Apple logo in one hand. "You were a real pain in the ass to find," she told me, as I took a seat across from her. I liked her immediately.

"Desiree spent the past three months helping me search L.A. for you," Carter explained, as he sat beside me. As the limo pulled away from the curb, he asked her, "Any news?"

She shook her head. "I have people watching the private jet terminals here at LAX and the four nearest municipal airports, and they haven't spotted the brothers' plane. Could be they're flying into an outlying airport, but there are too many of them to cover. I also have a team keeping an eye on the brothers' compound. So far today, no one's been in or out."

"We probably beat them here. I don't think they flew out of Belfast, or I would have seen their plane when I went to get the helicopter. That must mean they had a bit of a drive to another airport, which would have slowed them down. That's a good thing, since time is obviously of the essence." Carter glanced at me, then said, "Stop that, or you won't have a thumbnail left."

I forced myself to stop chewing on that same raggedy nail and asked, "Can I use your phone again?"

When he handed it over, I placed yet another call to Griffin. Like the six calls before it, this one went straight to voicemail. I'd called Ari several times as well, with the same result. I'd also called their hotel in Paris and had been told they'd checked out the day before. I had no idea what that was about, but I really hoped to hear back from them soon.

As I handed his phone back, I glanced out the window and asked, "Where are we headed?"

Carter said, "My house."

"We need to swing by mine first," I said. "I need my phone, which has a lot of Griffin's contacts in it. Maybe one of them knows how to reach him, because we really need his help."

"Not a problem." Carter lowered the privacy window and relayed the new address to his driver. Once the window was back in place, he asked, "How powerful is Griffin?"

"That's hard to say. He came into his powers last fall and is still learning how to use them. I don't think he knows what he's really capable of at this point."

Carter asked, "And he's what, a quarter warlock? Or maybe half?"

"More than that."

I had every intention of keeping my friend's secret, but I actually forgot Carter could read minds until he blurted, "He's a full-blooded warlock? I was sure they were all extinct."

I frowned at him and said, "Please keep that information to yourselves, both of you. You know how rare it is, and you also know there are plenty of people who'd love to exploit his power."

"I won't say a word, and neither will Desiree," Carter assured me.

Desiree looked up from her laptop and raised an eyebrow. "How the hell is there a full-blooded warlock left in the twenty-first century? Is he the result of centuries of inbreeding, or what?"

I frowned at her and said, "No. His parents both came from what had to be the last two unbroken magical dynasties in the world."

"And they just happened to meet and have a baby, while not being first cousins or some shit," she said flatly.

"Yes," I said. "Exactly."

She muttered, "Uh huh," and turned her attention back to the computer.

I stared out the window for a while as we rolled through L.A. It was light out and seemed to be early morning, but I'd lost all sense of time. After a while, I murmured, "What if we're wrong, and they stayed on the east coast? We just assumed they'd come back to L.A., but we don't really know that."

"Cain is definitely in his compound," Desiree said. "One of my people spotted him early this morning. Word on the street is, he was mega-pissed about the way Elias turned against him, and he's a real vindictive fucker. I'm sure he's going to want a piece of the torturing action, which means they're definitely bringing him back here."

"Okay. I mean, that's terrible, but at least we're in the right place."

She squinted at me and asked, "So, do you actually like your mate now? Because you spent the last century dodging his ass, but all of a sudden you're concerned about his well-being."

"Yes. I actually like my mate now."

Desiree looked impressed. "Well, damn. You must have gotten some good dick on that island to make a turn-around like that in twenty-four hours." I couldn't help but grin a little.

When we reached my house, Carter muttered, "Whose car is that?" A fully restored black 1970 Chevelle was parked next to my Barracuda.

I'd actually done some work on that car, so I told him, "That belongs to one of Griffin's friends."

Carter glanced at the house and said, "There are two vampires inside. Which reminds me, I forgot to restore your wards after I tore them apart."

A moment later, Griffin's friend Tinder flung open the front door, flashed me a smile, and asked, "Dude, where have you been? Griffin called out the cavalry thinking something bad happened to you. But here you are, rolling up in a limo with a beautiful woman and some guy who feels like the prince of darkness—which is totally badass, by the way."

Desiree hoisted a big handbag onto her shoulder and said, "I like this guy," as she preceded me up the stairs.

I asked, "When did you talk to Griffin?"

"Last night," Tinder said, as he pushed his dark hair out of his eyes. "He had a premonition of sorts and thought you might be in trouble, so he tried calling you. Your phone went right to voicemail and you didn't answer the land line, so he asked August and me to check on you. When we got here, we discovered your wards were all fucked up, and the place gave off this weird energy. The whole thing felt like a supernatural crime scene, so we called Griffin and Ari back, and they hopped on the first available flight."

"Really? They're on their way back from France?" When Tinder nodded, I murmured, "Thank god."

As we all went into the house, he asked, "What's going on?"

Meanwhile, Desiree stuck her head in the pastel, floral living room and muttered, "Christ almighty. It looks like a whole pack of old white ladies threw up in here."

"Let's go back to the den," I said, "and I'll explain everything. I'm replying to Tinder, by the way, not justifying my home decor."

She turned to the vampire and raised a brow. "Why are you named after a dating app?"

He grinned at her. "I was named way before the app existed. My real name's Tyler, but my brother gave me the nickname when we were kids, because it was so easy to ignite my temper."

"Okay, that's good," she said, as she started down the hallway. "I had some concerns for a minute there, but you're alright."

We found Tinder's husband in the kitchen, perusing the bottles of wine on the table. "August and Tinder, meet Desiree and Carter," I said. "She's a witch and he's a demon, in case you were wondering. Carter, these are the two vampire-warlock hybrids I mentioned."

"Fascinating," August said, as he stepped forward and shook Carter's hand. "I've never met a demon before."

Desiree glared at him and asked, "What am I, chopped liver?"

"Apologies," August said, laying on the charm as he took her hand. He kissed the back of it, then said, "I was momentarily distracted by your unique counterpart, but let me make it up to you. Would you like a glass of Mateo's strikingly mediocre wine?"

"I guess I forgive you, mostly because you're fine. You look and sound like that English dude who plays Lucifer on TV. And yes, I would like some wine. I'll take the rosé, and I'll be in there. It seems to be the only room in this place that wasn't decorated by a geriatric sister-wife." She went into the den with Carter while August unscrewed the lid on the rosé.

While he poured the wine, I explained the situation to August and his husband as concisely as I could. When I finished, Tinder said, "We've been hearing some pretty gruesome rumors about a pair of demons over the last couple of months, everything from enslaving humans to killing vampires for sport. We haven't found any actual witnesses though, so it's tough to know how much to believe."

We joined Desiree and Carter, and as August handed her a glass of wine, he asked us, "So, any ideas on how to rescue Mateo's partner without actually dying?"

"Someone could sneak in and try to get him out while the rest of us cause a distraction," Tinder said, as he sat down right beside his husband on the sofa and August put an arm around his shoulders. They were an interesting couple. Tinder was as rough around the edges as August was sophisticated, but somehow they seemed perfect together.

Desiree had opened her laptop again, and I asked, "Do you need my wi-fi password?"

Her laugh came out as a snort. "Please. I'm on witch-fi. I don't need a damn password."

I glanced at her screen as a series of six live feeds came up, and I asked, "Is that the brothers' compound?"

"Yeah. It's actually not far from here, up on Skyview Road. There are two gates, both with armed guards, and the whole thing's surrounded by a ten-foot brick wall. That's just ridiculous, since it's also warded." She drained her wine glass and handed it to August without a word, and he jumped up to refill it.

I asked, "How are we going to get around the wards? As soon as we start chipping away at them it'll alert the brothers, and there goes any hope of catching them by surprise."

Desiree gestured at the screen as a delivery van pulled up to the gate. It had the name of a local butcher shop on the side, and it was waved through by the guards. "We need some kind of Trojan horse situation, like all y'all crammed in the back of a catering truck or some shit."

I asked, "Why didn't you include yourself in that scenario?"

"Because I'm the guy in the chair."

"The what?"

She stared at me like I was thick. "The guy in the chair. Or in this case, the woman, but in sexist action movies it's always a guy. In other words, you need someone on the outside, acting as your eyes, monitoring the situation, and feeding you information. That's me."

Something occurred to me, and I asked, "Wait, why are the brothers having food delivered? Do demons even eat?"

"We can if we choose to. It's not mandatory, but sometimes it's nice." Carter leaned over to get a look at the computer screen. "Here comes another delivery van. I think they're hosting a dinner party."

I frowned at that. "So, they're taking a break from torture and mayhem to throw a soiree? Really?"

"Everything the brothers do is for their own amusement," Carter explained. "The problem with living for millennia is the tedium. Every day is just like the next, and it stretches on in this endless cycle of monotony. So, here on earth, they're going to do whatever they find entertaining. That could definitely include a dinner party for, let's say, the most notorious criminals on the west coast, followed by a live show of the brothers torturing their enemies. It would certainly drive the point home that they're never to be crossed."

The part about torture made me nauseous. What if that was exactly what they were planning, now that they'd captured Elias?

When August returned with her glass of wine, Desiree said, "Thank you, Lucifer," and took a drink.

"August," he corrected her.

"Whatever. I've already forgotten your husband's name, but I know it was a dating app. I'm just gonna call him Grinder." She said that in all seriousness, and Tinder burst out laughing.

"Going back to what you were saying before, the Trojan horse idea isn't bad," Carter said. "Neither is the idea of trying to cause a distraction while one of us sneaks in, since those gates obviously allow access past the wards. I really don't think we stand a chance if we go for a frontal assault."

"So, let's blow up part of their compound while Carter goes in and gets Elias," Desiree said, as she clicked on the keys with her glitter-polished nails. "After that, we should all plan on leaving the country ASAP, because the brothers are going to be *pissed*."

I said, "Carter's not going in to get him. I am."

"I'll be much more capable of defending myself if I'm discovered," he told me.

I held his gaze steadily. "But Elias is mine, so I'm going in after him."

"You know," Tinder said, as he adjusted the collar of his black leather jacket, "Desiree's right. The brothers are going to be furious if we rescue Elias, and there's probably nowhere on earth we could hide from something that powerful."

I asked, "So, what are you saying?"

Tinder turned to Carter and asked, "Can demons die?"

"We can be destroyed," he said. "It's not easy, but it is possible. It would take…well, the magical equivalent of an atomic bomb, I guess."

"The only way to make sure we survive this is to destroy at least one of the brothers. If those rumors are true, then they need killing anyway," Tinder said, and Desiree nodded in agreement. Those two were both remarkably matter-of-fact about the idea of destroying demons and blowing shit up, as if they did this every day.

I asked, "How do you propose we do that?"

"Divide and conquer," he told me. "We can't take both of them down at once, since you said they multiply each other's powers. So, we lure one away, then hit the other with everything we've got. That should work, right? All of us plus Carter should add up to more power than either brother has on his own."

"Theoretically," Carter muttered, as he absently adjusted his tie. He was in another black-on-black mafioso-inspired suit, shirt, and tie combo, which meant he and August were dressed identically. I probably would have found that funny if worry wasn't eating away at my gut.

I ran both hands over my hair and asked, "When are Griffin and Ari arriving?"

"Around eight this evening," Tinder said.

"Shit," I muttered. "I don't know if Elias has that much time."

"You know, we're not the only people on earth who can work magic," August chimed in. "If the stories we've been hearing are true, the brothers pose a huge threat across the board, so it's in everyone's interest to take them down. What if we put out a call and try to assemble everyone with magical ability in Southern Califor-nia? The more people we gather, the more powerful we become."

"Two problems with that," Desiree said. "First of all, it takes time to build an army, and for Elias's sake we need to act fast. Also, as soon as you start putting out the call for help, you run the risk of word getting back to the brothers. If they find out we're plotting against them and trying to pull off a rescue mission, the first thing they'll do is kill Elias. Then they'll probably come after us with guns blazing."

"She's right," I muttered, rubbing my temples as a headache brewed. "I need a few minutes to myself, but please keep talking strategy. I'll be back soon."

I went down the hall to my room and shut the door behind me, and then I exhaled slowly. I didn't want to stop moving, because I knew as soon as I did, fear, exhaustion, and worry would overwhelm me. So, just because it was something to keep me occupied, I stripped and stood under a hot shower for a few minutes.

After I toweled off, I got dressed in jeans, a black, long-sleeved T-shirt, and sneakers. At the same time, I listened to the conversation down the hall. My breath caught when Desiree said, "Heads up, boys. A black SUV just pulled up to the gate at the compound. I think I see—yeah, the driver just rolled down a window, and Abel's in the passenger seat. I can't see Elias with that tinted glass, but I'm willing to bet he's in back."

"We need to finalize a plan, and fast," Carter said. "How can we do this while making sure we all survive?"

In that moment, I made a decision—I was going to rescue Elias myself. I couldn't wait for them to reach a consensus, and I didn't want them to risk their lives when I might be able to do this on my own. The last thing the brothers would expect was one little idiot sneaking onto their property. Maybe I could slip in, get my mate, and slip out again. It didn't have to turn into a huge showdown, which our side would definitely lose.

I cast the strongest concealment spell on myself that I could muster, which should keep the brothers from sensing me if I made it inside the compound. Then I slipped out the window and ran down the hill. Once I reached the street, I looked around frantically. After a minute, I spotted a vintage, white van which read "Filly's Flowers" and stepped in front of it, waving my arms.

The young, redhaired woman behind the wheel slammed on the

brakes. Then she rolled down her window and exclaimed, "You need to be more careful! I almost hit you."

I made myself calm down enough to use my Jedi mind trick and said, "I need to borrow your van."

She blinked at me, then murmured, "Okay," and climbed out of the driver's seat.

"Go treat yourself to a nice afternoon off," I said. "Maybe buy a cookie."

"I like cookies," she mumbled, as she wandered away.

I got behind the wheel and took a deep breath. Then I threw the van into gear and slammed on the gas. Not much happened since the thing was about fifty years old, so I uttered a spell that sent it shooting forward like a rocket.

"I'm coming, Elias," I whispered, though he obviously couldn't hear me. "You're going to be so mad when you find out I put myself in harm's way, but you're everything to me, and I can't let them hurt you."

Chapter 9

It was easy enough to find the compound once I reached Skyview Road. I sensed Elias's presence when I was within half a mile of him, and my heart began to race. Soon after, I spotted that huge wall.

I scribbled down the address and a note on a clipboard, then pulled up to the back gate, shielding my face with one hand when I passed the spot where Desiree's hidden camera must be. They were probably all watching this right now, and I hoped they didn't recognize me and decide to come and help.

When a mountain of a guard approached me, I said, "Delivery."

"You're not on my list."

I picked up the clipboard and pointed at the stuff I'd just written. "Well, you're on mine. It's right here, four centerpieces." He scowled at me, and a long moment ticked by. I didn't expect my mind trick to work on someone whose job it was to guard a demonic compound, but I tried it anyway, concentrating as I said, "Look again, I'm on your list."

Surprisingly, he did as I asked, then stepped back and pushed a button to open the iron gate. The brothers must not be particularly concerned about security, not if it was that easy to compel their guards. Then again, who would be dumb enough to break in here?

"Park by the kitchen, second building on the right," the guard told me. "Then use the service entrance."

I exhaled slowly as I rolled through the gate. Ahead of me were several attractive, Spanish-style buildings with white stucco walls and terra cotta tile roofs, surrounded by perfectly maintained landscaping. I didn't know what I'd been expecting, but it definitely wasn't this. It was hard to tell what it had been before the brothers took over, but if I had to guess I'd say it was a private school of some sort.

I parked by the kitchen and opened the back of the van, then selected the largest floral arrangement and carried it into the building. There were several red aprons hanging on hooks by the back door, so I put one on, pushed my sleeves back, and picked up the flowers again.

Eight humans were in the kitchen, and none of them so much as glanced at me. Most were cooking. One was putting away a mop and bucket. It was eerily silent, and everyone was just zoned out. That was the only way to describe it. There was no expression on their faces, and their motions were slow and deliberate, almost mechanical. When I realized they were all bespelled, a sick feeling joined the knot of worry in my stomach.

I tried to pull up a blank expression as I walked through the kitchen and out the door at the other end, following Elias's pull. He'd sensed my presence, and he was terrified, angry, and overwhelmed with pain. My god, what had they done to him?

One thought rang out clearly above the chaos of his emotions. In fact, he was screaming it at me—*no, Mateo, get out of here!* I wasn't going to argue with him, but I obviously wasn't going to obey him, ether. This was too important.

When I came to a laundry room, I exchanged the flowers for a large canvas hamper on wheels and tossed in a few bedsheets. I kept up my poker face and tried to remain calm as I cut through the rest of that building, then another. Along the way, I passed two more bespelled humans who were cleaning. They didn't react to me at all.

The brothers were probably somewhere in the compound, but I was afraid to reach out and try to locate them. If I did that, they might sense it, so I just had to hope I didn't accidentally run into them.

Elias was in the third building I came to, near the center of the compound. The outer door was locked, but not warded. The brothers were obviously confident no one would be poking around, so maybe I was right about being able to fly under the radar.

I took care of the lock with a flick of my fingers, then pushed the hamper into a long hallway and closed the door behind me. All along the left side of the hallway were a series of closed doors, spaced about ten feet apart. Classrooms, or a dormitory, maybe? It was hard to tell.

My senses told me there was only one person in this building— Elias. I left the hamper and sprinted down the hall.

When I unlocked the unfurnished, windowless room where they were keeping him and stepped inside, my heart leapt into my throat. He was sprawled on the floor in an awkward position, his limbs twisted and broken. I whispered, "Oh god, Elias," as I ran to his side and fell to my knees.

I brushed my hand over his forehead, and a tear tumbled down my cheek as I whispered a spell to ease his pain. People with magical ability could usually sense magic when it was being used, but hope- fully it was small enough that the brothers wouldn't notice. "You have to get out of here," he whispered. "Please. Don't let them catch you."

"We're both getting out of here."

"No. Leave me and save yourself," he rasped. "I'm begging you."

"You're my mate." I caressed his cheek, which was rough with razor stubble. "You're the most important thing in the world to me, and there's absolutely no way on earth I'm leaving you here. We live or die together. That's just the way it is."

The lines of agony on his face softened, and his eyes closed as the incantation did its job. He needed a healing spell, but that would take a lot of time and magic, and I was already pushing my luck. I picked him up carefully, thanking the universe for the extra strength my werewolf side provided, and carried him out of the room and down the hall.

I put him in the hamper as gently as I could and covered him with the sheets. This had to be the oldest trick in the book for sneaking someone out of a building, but it was exactly what I needed right now.

It took every ounce of restraint I had to wheel that cart slowly and calmly through the compound, while everything in me was urging me to run. My heart was trying to beat its way out of my chest, and I hoped my luck would hold for just a few more minutes.

Thankfully, I made it past all those bespelled humans and back to the parking lot without incident. Then I opened the back of the van, picked up the hamper, and slid it inside, pushing aside several arrangements and buckets of flowers in the process.

Fear shot through me when I heard someone say, "Why would a florist be loading laundry into the back of their van?"

Two guards in black uniforms had rounded the far corner of the building. They were maybe twenty yards away, and when they both began striding toward me with grim expressions, I tried to plant the idea in their minds to head in the opposite direction. Either they were shielded against magic or I was too panicked to concentrate, but it didn't work.

I slammed the back door, then ran around the van and climbed behind the wheel as they yelled at me to stop. No fucking way was that going to happen. They ran toward me as one of them spoke into a walkie talkie. Meanwhile, I started the engine, threw it into reverse, and swung around in a wide arc. When one of them pulled a gun, I flung my arm and yanked it out of his hand. Then I threw the van into gear and slammed on the gas pedal.

The gate was about a hundred yards away, and it was shut. I wondered if this old van had enough juice to ram it, since I was rapidly burning up my energy and it would take a lot to knock it down.

As I sped closer, the guard who'd let me in stepped out of the kiosk with a giant fucking automatic rifle. I swept my arm and sent him rolling like a tumbleweed, and then I drew a sharp breath as a gunshot rang out behind me.

The bullet hit one of my tires, and the van listed to the left and slammed into a parked car. I was thrown around from the impact, and I cried out as my forehead struck the steering wheel.

I ignored the instant headache and the blood that began streaming down the side of my face as I threw the van in reverse. The tires spun when I stepped on the gas. It had gotten hung up on the other car and wasn't going anywhere.

I tumbled out the door, and as I ran to the back of the van, I spotted a guard who was aiming a gun at me. When I shoved my hand forward, he fell backwards, and his shot whizzed past my right ear. I threw open the back door and pulled the hamper to the ground with a sweeping gesture. Then I gathered Elias in my arms and began to run.

It took a lot out of me when I yelled an incantation that ripped the iron gate off its hinges and sent it clattering to the ground. The moment I did that, the wards around the compound flared with blue light and began swinging shut across the opening in the fence. I strained to hold them apart, shaking from the effort. Another pair of guards were running toward me on my right, and I cried out from the strain as I knocked them over with a flick of my wrist.

The rift I was struggling to hold open looked like a little sliver of clear sky between two huge walls of blue static. I'd almost totally depleted my energy, and my body was shaking. Meanwhile, the gap was getting narrower and narrower, and I was growing weaker by the second.

I wasn't going to make it.

The gap narrowed to just three or four inches, and I fell to my knees and cradled Elias to my chest. I poured everything I had into holding those walls of energy apart, because once they closed, we were trapped. I was too stubborn to let it go, but I knew I didn't have enough strength left to open them enough to slip through.

"I'm so sorry," I whispered into Elias's ear, as my body trembled and tears and blood streamed down my face. "I thought I could save you. God, I'm sorry."

In the next instant, a shiny, black Chevelle pulled up alongside the opening in the fence. Carter jumped out of the car and thrust both hands in front of him, then pulled them apart. The gap between the walls of energy widened to about three feet, and from behind the wheel, Tinder yelled, "Run, Mateo!"

I struggled to my feet and somehow found the strength to carry Elias to safety. Behind me, people were shouting as I clambered over the flattened gate.

As soon as I stepped through the gap, Carter let the wards slam shut. I glanced behind me as a barrage of bullets hit the now-invisible wall of energy and fell to the ground.

Carter flipped up the passenger seat and I slid in behind it, collapsing onto the backseat with Elias. The demon barely had a chance to sit down and close the door before Tinder slammed on the gas.

As we pulled away with a squeal of rubber on asphalt, I glanced into the compound. A tall man with shoulder-length white hair had just stepped out of one of the buildings. Even across a distance of more than a hundred yards, he managed to lock eyes with me. Then he smiled, and it sent a trickle of fear down my spine. Somehow, I just knew he was one of the brothers, and that smile was a promise he'd be seeing me soon.

Carter turned to me and frowned as we sped down the street. He closed the wound on my forehead with a small gesture, and I took off the apron and used it to wipe the blood, tears, and sweat off my face as he asked, "How's Elias?"

"They broke his arms and legs. I used a spell to ease his pain and let him rest, but I don't have enough energy left to heal him. Can you do it?"

He reached back and rested a hand on his friend's chest as he said, "I have to think about how to do this. It's pretty far outside my usual skill set."

He knit his brows in concentration. Elias was still out, but I soon felt his body shifting in my arms. After maybe a minute, Carter removed his hand and said, "It's done. He should be okay now." I thanked him and ran my hand over Elias's hair.

Tinder glanced in the rearview mirror and said, "We have company."

As the Chevy began to accelerate, I glanced over my shoulder and spotted a black Porsche Carrera gaining fast. I asked, "Are either of the brothers in that car?"

Carter shook his head, and then he gestured at the sports car. "It's just a couple of their lackeys, but the car's bespelled, so I can't knock out its engine. We'll have to lose them."

Tinder grinned and said, "On it. You might want to hold onto something," as he shifted gears. The muscle car surged forward.

Carter asked him, "Can I assume your license plate leads to a dead-end, or will we have to worry because the brothers know who you are now?"

"It's registered to a fake name and address in Burbank, so no worries there," Tinder said, as he shifted gears. Of course it was. My plates were registered to a phony name and address in Pasadena. Most nonhumans knew to fly under the radar, which meant avoiding things like the DMV.

As Tinder dodged around a car ahead of us at about seventy miles an hour, I held Elias securely and asked, "Where are Desiree and August?"

"We split into two groups," Carter explained, grabbing the handle above the door as Tinder flung the car around a corner with a screech of tires. Once we were on the straightaway again, Carter continued, "They went around to the front of the complex and were prepared to cause a distraction if we needed one. They borrowed your Barracuda, by the way, since that was the only other car at the house. Now they're headed to Tinder and August's place up the coast, which is where we'll rendezvous with them once we lose the Porsche."

I asked, "Who picked the teams?"

"You mean, why didn't Tinder and his husband pair up? That was Desiree's doing. She said something about eye candy and insisted on working with August," Carter explained, as he tried to push a parked car into our pursuers' path. When it instantly swung out of the way, he muttered, "At least one of the people chasing us is part warlock."

Tinder changed lanes suddenly, which made me grab the seat in front of me. "I assume this car's warded," I said. "Otherwise, they probably would have already disabled our engine or thrown a truck at us or something."

"Yup. Carter thought to ward both cars before we left your house," Tinder said. The Chevelle's powerful engine revved, and he switched gears again as he wove through traffic. The fact that he was grinning and clearly enjoying this told me a lot about him.

I asked, "Did you know what I was doing because you spotted me on Desiree's video feed?"

"Yes," Carter said, "and it was a terrible idea to attempt this without us. You need to learn it's okay to rely on someone other than yourself."

He was right. My rescue mission had almost ended in disaster. It was terrifying to think about what might have happened if my friends hadn't shown up when they did.

My mate stirred in my arms just then, raising his eyelids partway as he murmured, "Mateo."

"Hi." I caressed his cheek and asked, "How do you feel?"

Elias sat up and looked around. "Groggy, but aside from that I feel good. Did you heal me?"

"Carter did. I didn't have any juice left after my nearly catastrophic attempt at smuggling you out of the compound."

He squeezed his friend's shoulder as he said, "Thanks, Carter." Then he asked me, "What happened after you put me under?"

After I told him the story and introduced him to Tinder, Elias frowned at me and muttered, "You're getting such a spanking for endangering yourself like that." My cock twitched, and of course everyone in the car sensed my arousal. Tinder chuckled, and Carter glanced at us, then quickly looked away. Who knew it was that easy to embarrass a demon?

We all braced ourselves as Tinder took a wild left through a red light. Horns blared and brakes squealed, but somehow no one collided. That was followed by an almost immediate right. A few seconds later, he slowed down and glanced in the rearview mirror. "I lost them," he said with a smirk. "Amateurs."

Carter sent a text and got one in return moments later. "Desiree and August got away without incident." He put his phone down and murmured, "I suppose this could have gone far worse."

"It's not over, though," I said. "We have to stop the brothers. I don't know how, but it has to be done, and not just because they're after Elias. I saw one of them as we were leaving. He and I locked eyes, and it was absolutely chilling. Evil just radiated from him. Also, there are all these humans working at the compound, and I think they're bespelled and being kept there against their will."

Elias asked, "Which brother did you see?"

"I don't know. He had white hair."

"That's Cain. I'm surprised you got away, if he was close enough to make eye contact."

"Actually, we weren't close at all," I said. "I was in the car, just outside the gate, and he stepped out of one of the buildings a moment before we sped off. Somehow though, he let me know he saw me, really *saw me*, and it was disturbing."

Elias sighed. "I'm sure you're as high up on their hit list as I am now. They won't take someone breaking into their home lightly."

"I would have ended up on their list anyway, as soon as they figured out you had a mate."

"This is different, though. Now they'll actively be gunning for you."

After a pause, I asked, "Since the brothers just tracked Elias to a tiny island on the east coast, what's to prevent them from showing up at Tinder's house?"

"I've been giving a lot of thought to how they found him in Maine," Carter said, "and it had to come down to tracking me. Until today, I don't think they knew you existed, so I'm the only explanation. I've already strengthened and recast the concealment spells I had on myself and Elias. The brothers shouldn't be able to track us, at least not by any means I can think of."

"Good idea," I said. "But even if they can't track us using

magic, they can still use more conventional methods, like hacking into traffic cams."

Carter nodded. "The protection spell I cast on both cars also renders them invisible to any cameras they pass." He really was remarkably thorough.

After a pause, I said, "I owe a company called Filly's Flowers a new delivery van, plus some money for all the arrangements I ruined today. I need—"

Carter picked up his phone and started composing a text as he said, "Consider it done."

"No, you don't have to do anything. I was just saying I'll need to get to my money, which is mostly cash, so—"

He cut me off again as he put the phone in his pocket. "It's already taken care of. They'll be receiving a huge check this afternoon, which will more than cover the damages."

"You didn't have to do that."

"I know. I wanted to."

"Thank you, Carter," I said. "I owe you so much, including my life, and Elias's, and now this."

"You don't owe me anything," he muttered. "Friends take care of each other. That's just how it goes."

"You really are a great friend," I told him. He seemed to like hearing that.

Eventually, we reached Tinder and August's sprawling, mission-style ranch house, which was located on several acres along an empty stretch of coast north of L.A. It felt remarkably isolated for Southern California.

Tinder parked in the massive, detached garage, and he and Carter got out of the car and began discussing the wards on the house. Meanwhile, I climbed out of the backseat and waited for Elias. He tried out one leg, then the other before putting his weight on them, and I asked, "How are you doing?"

"Surprisingly well," he said, as he straightened up. "I'm tired, but whatever Carter did to heal me seems to have worked wonders."

I wrapped my arms around him, and we held each other for a long moment as he kissed my forehead and whispered, "When they took me from the island, I was so scared I'd never see you again."

"You had to know I'd come for you."

"I knew you'd try, no matter what I did to stop you, but I thought they'd kill me before you found me." He leaned back and searched my face as he asked, "How angry are you about that potion back on the island?"

"I couldn't be mad at you right now if I tried. At some point, we need to talk about learning to make decisions as a couple. But today, I just want to celebrate getting you back."

A moment later, my Barracuda pulled into the garage. August climbed out of the driver's seat, pulled his husband close, and planted a rough, demanding kiss on him. Then Tinder grinned and said, "I missed you, too."

August asked him, "Did you have any trouble?"

"There was a minor car chase. Nothing I couldn't handle."

They kissed again, and August picked up Tinder and sat him on the Chevelle's fender. Then he seemed to remember the rest of us existed and said, "Go on in and make yourselves comfortable. The wards will let you through. Take any of the guestrooms on the ground floor if you want to get some rest. I don't think there's any food, but there's plenty of alcohol. We'll join you in a little while, but first I need to fuck my husband."

"He's got his priorities straight," Desiree said, as she led the way out of the garage.

As we followed her to the house, I asked, "Can I borrow your phone?"

Desiree pulled my phone from her purse and handed it to me as she said, "I saw this at your house while you were off pretending to be Batman, and I figured you'd need it if you failed to die."

I thanked her and charged it by tapping it with my finger. She unlocked the front door with a flick of her wrist, and as we followed her inside, I sent a text to Griffin and Ari so they'd know where we were once their flight landed.

Desiree said, "I'm going to find the liquor cabinet. Who's with me?"

Carter stepped around us and told her, "I am."

"Elias should rest, so I'm taking him to bed," I said, and we turned left and headed down the hall. "We'll see you in a few hours. Don't wake us unless it's a matter of life and death."

The house was warm and inviting, with beamed ceilings, arched doorways, and Spanish tile floors. I selected a cozy room at the very end of the hall, and Elias and I both stripped to our briefs before climbing under the covers and wrapping ourselves around each other. I exhaled slowly, shuddering a little as the last of the adrenaline drained away. We fell asleep within minutes.

Chapter 10

Several hours later, I woke with a start and sat up in bed. It took me a few moments to figure out where I was and what was happening. My sudden movement woke Elias, and he reached for me as he murmured, "Bad dream?"

"No. I just felt a little disoriented for a minute there." I curled into him, and he wrapped himself around me. After a while, I said, "Our mate bond feels different to me. That mania has gone away. Has it changed for you, too?"

He nodded. "It's because we finally had sex and cemented the bond. Until we did that, it was always going to feel frantic and out of control."

"This is wonderful," I murmured, as I burrowed deeper into his arms. "I'm not used to feeling so secure."

After another pause, he asked, "Do you think you might trust me with the story of your life before we met? I feel like I'm missing a big piece of the puzzle when it comes to really knowing you."

I tucked my head under his chin. "I'll only tell you my story if you promise not to pity me. You also have to promise not to ask a bunch of follow-up questions. I just want to put it out there and be done with it."

He kissed the top of my head and whispered, "I promise."

I took a deep breath and tried to leave the emotion out of it as I began to speak. If I just told him the facts, maybe it wouldn't hurt as much. "I was raised by a cold, domineering man who had nothing but contempt for me. My mom died during childbirth, and he adored her. There was a huge portrait of her in our home, and he always kept candles burning and fresh flowers beneath it. If he's still alive, I'd bet anything he's still maintaining that altar."

I shifted my position, holding onto Elias tightly as I continued, "His love for his wife was obsessive, and he blamed me for taking her away from him. Most people would realize that was irrational, but he was the type of person who had to blame someone for everything, so I became his scapegoat.

"He feared me, too, which was probably why he was so determined to control me. I'd inherited my powers from my mom, and he was a half-werewolf, half-human with no magical abilities. I think he was worried I'd eventually realize my strength and become a threat to him, so I was forbidden to use magic. But I was a kid, and I was curious.

"When I was eleven, I found my mom's spell book and snuck out to the barn to see if I could actually do any of the things it described. Not really, it turned out, since witches and warlocks don't fully come into their power until they turn twenty-five. I also couldn't control what little power I had, because no one ever taught me how. So, in the process of trying to work a simple illumination spell, I ended up catching the barn on fire.

"My father made his living as a horse breeder. I barely made it out alive, because I made sure I got every single horse out safely. By the time I stumbled out of the barn, my father and a few of his ranch hands had arrived. The men took one look at the fire, which was burning with blue flames, and they made the sign of the cross and yelled, "*El diablo!*" This was over a century ago in rural Mexico, and a lot of people were pretty superstitious. I think they really believed I was the devil, or maybe some sort of demon, and they grabbed anything they could use as a weapon and started to come after me.

"I begged my father to tell them I wasn't evil. He knew his wife had been half witch, so he knew what I was. But I guess he was afraid the men would turn on him too, so he sided with them and called me a demon. I had to run for my life." My voice shook at that last part.

I paused for a few moments to try to get my emotions under control again. Then I continued, "I knew I could never go home again, so from that point forward, I was on my own. All I had at first were the clothes on my back. I'd even lost my mom's spell book in the fire. But I managed to escape to northern Mexico by hiding in the back of a wagon, and then I learned to survive. I grew up and got stronger, and I dreamed of building a new life in the U.S., the land of opportunity. Right before I turned twenty, I finally made my dream come true and moved to California."

"And then you met me, and the first thing I did was try to control you," Elias said softly.

"You didn't know what I'd been through."

After a pause, he asked, "How did you survive all those years on your own? You were so young, and—sorry. I promised not to ask a bunch of questions."

"It's okay, I'll answer that one. I begged in the streets, but only at first. Pretty soon, I realized it was up to me to make something of myself, and I wanted to be more than just a street rat. I took any odd job I could get, saved some of the money I made, and worked toward my dream of a fresh start in America."

"Did your powers help you survive?"

"Not really. I was afraid to use them after the fire, and in the years that followed. Also, when I realized I could read minds and plant suggestions, I was worried about taking advantage of people, so I didn't use those abilities, either. It's always been important to me to be respectful of my mother's memory. She's the reason I have these powers, and I'm sure she would have wanted me to do the right thing."

After a few moments, I added, "I guess I also wanted to prove I wasn't evil, despite what my father and our ranch hands had said. They all knew me, Elias. They helped raise me from the time I was a baby, and then they turned on me. I almost expected it from my father, because I knew he hated me. But I didn't expect it from the rest of them." I met his gaze and asked, "Now do you see why I've always felt I couldn't rely on anyone but myself?"

"I do, and I'm sorry I was so awful when we met. I didn't give you a single reason to trust me."

"It was all just bad timing," I said. "I wasn't ready for a mate back then, and you were still in mourning. My only regrets are the decades we lost, and the fact that I channeled my fear and insecurity into anger. That wasn't fair to you."

"Your anger was justified."

"It was an excuse to push you away." I stretched up and kissed him before saying, "I just realized we're violating our rule about focusing on the present instead of the past."

"This was important though, and I'm grateful you confided in me. I know it wasn't easy to talk about what happened to you."

"It doesn't feel right to keep secrets from you, not when you're a part of me."

"A part you never asked for."

"But a part I'm definitely learning to appreciate."

He grinned and said, "It's nice to be appreciated."

I just had to ask. "Would you have chosen me as your mate? You know, if you didn't have to?"

"Again and again and again."

"Even though I'm stubborn and disobedient?"

His grin turned devious. "That's not so bad. It gives me plenty of reasons to spank you."

I grinned, too. "Do you really need a reason?"

"No, I suppose I don't." Elias kissed my forehead and climbed out of bed. "This is going to seem like an abrupt subject change, but I'm going to take a shower. After that, I'd love to get to some of that spanking, followed by a lot of fucking. But first, I want to wash the scent of the compound off of me."

"Can I join you?"

"I was just about to extend an invitation."

I followed him into the bathroom, and after we stripped down and stepped under the hot water, we took turns washing each other. It started out all business, because I was determined to scrub him thoroughly after that comment about the compound. Even so, by the time I got to his cock, it was rock hard. I soaped it up before massaging his balls, and a low growl of pure lust rumbled in his throat.

He took the soap from me and went to work. When he turned his attention to my ass and slipped a soapy finger inside me, I moaned and leaned against him. I wanted him to fuck me right then and there, but he had other plans.

Once we were both clean—and totally worked up—we stepped out of the shower and quickly dried off. Then we returned to the bedroom, and Elias steered me to the long, wooden dresser instead of the bed. He picked up the end of the heavy piece of furniture and angled it away from the wall, and when I turned to look at him, he kissed me tenderly. "That's for coming to rescue me." Then he frowned and said, "This next part is for endangering yourself in the process. Bend over the dresser."

"I'll always rescue you, no matter how many times you tell me not to." I flashed him a big smile and added, "Also, you know spanking me is a reward and not a punishment, right?"

"Let's just call it symbolically punishing you, even if you get off on it."

"Works for me."

The dresser was a little tall for me, so I had to stand on my toes in order to bend over it. I held on to the edges and rested my cheek against the cool, smooth surface, and Elias massaged my ass before bringing his hand down on it. My cock twitched in response.

He took his time, spanking me until my butt was warm and red. I drifted along on all that sensation, savoring the caresses to my sore ass between the spanks. Now and then, he reached around and stroked my cock, always leaving me wanting more. I loved every minute of it.

When he decided I'd had enough, he stepped back and told me, "Climb up on the dresser. I want you on your back with your legs spread."

I complied immediately, hooking my hands behind the backs of my knees once I got into position. He grabbed my hips and slid me to the edge of the dresser, so my ass hung over by a few inches. Then he surprised me by dropping to his knees and running his tongue along my crack.

It was so intimate and unexpected that I started to sit up, but he met my gaze and said, quietly but with authority, "You're not getting up until I give you permission. Understood?" I nodded and settled back down.

He licked my crack again and lapped at my hole while I tried not to squirm. Then he slid his tongue into me, and I moaned as my cock throbbed.

"Please, can I?" My words came out choppy and desperate. Somehow he knew what I meant. He grasped the backs of my thighs and pushed my legs up and apart, freeing my hands so I could jerk myself off.

He licked and sucked and tongue-fucked my asshole while I worked my cock fast and hard. It was almost too much—all that pleasure, all that sensation, combined with the warm throb of my spanked ass. The fact that I was on the dresser instead of the bed just added to it. I was on display for him, served up for his pleasure.

I was just about to drive myself over the edge when he said, "You don't come until I give you permission. Understand?" I whimpered, but then I forced myself to let go of my cock, and he murmured, "That's very good, *mi amor*."

He went back to eating my ass while I moaned and leaked precum and uselessly bucked my hips, desperate for friction but thrusting into thin air. When he ran his tongue over my balls and up my shaft, the sound I made was close to a sob of relief.

Elias took my cockhead in his mouth and sucked hard, then let go of it. He then proceeded to drive me right to the brink of orgasm and pull me back, again and again. It was the most exquisite agony I could ever imagine.

My cock was rock-hard, aching, throbbing, as he licked and sucked me, stroked me, fingered me. I arched off the dresser, crying out as he took me to the edge again, sucking my balls as his fingers pushed into my ass and massaged my prostate. "Please, Eli," I begged, when I thought I was about to lose my mind. "Please. I need to come."

Finally, *finally*, he said, "Go ahead, baby. Come for me," and wrapped his lips around my cock.

I yelled as I exploded down his throat, my entire body convulsing as wave after wave of that massive orgasm destroyed me. Moans that were more like sobs tore from me as I fucked his mouth. I grabbed his head with both hands, my legs over his shoulders as he swallowed me whole. I couldn't think, couldn't even see as that orgasm just kept rolling through me, taking everything I had.

By the time it finally ebbed, I was shattered. My body went limp as I gasped for breath, still splayed out on that dresser. Elias picked me up and cradled me against his chest as he carried me across the room. He felt so good—solid and strong and warm. I nestled against him, and he climbed into bed, leaning against the pillows with me on his lap.

When I could manage to string a sentence together, I whispered, "What about you?"

"I enjoyed every minute of that."

"But you didn't get to finish."

"Next time. This time, I just wanted to focus on you," he said.

I wove my fingers with his and drifted along for a while, tired and content and happy. Eventually, I murmured, "Tell me something no one else knows about you."

"Like what?"

"Anything at all. I want to know everything about you, Eli."

"Here's something no one knows about me. I'm a musician."

I looked up at him and asked, "What instrument do you play?"

"Several, but the piano is my favorite."

"Will you play for me sometime?"

He nodded. "You're the only person I'd play for."

"Don't you like performing for an audience?"

"I can't stand it," he said.

"Why is that?"

"Performing strips me bare." He rested our joined hands on his chest, and after a moment he said, "My mother taught me to play. She was an incredible singer and musician. I associate it so strongly with her memory that it's become a very personal thing."

I asked, very softly, "What happened to your parents?"

"They were murdered by a hunter who discovered they were both part werewolf."

"Oh god."

"My mother was an opera singer and my father was a painter. You'd never meet two kinder, gentler souls," he said. "But there have always been people who believe our kind is inherently evil, and who've tried to hunt us to extinction."

"How was their secret discovered?"

"Take a guess. Who'd be able to recognize someone with were-wolf blood?"

"Someone who was also part werewolf?" When he nodded, I exclaimed, "That's barbaric! He was hunting his own kind. How could anyone do that?"

"Self-hate, maybe? I don't know. I didn't bother to ask."

I met his gaze and asked, "Did you kill him?"

"Yes. He had to pay for what he did."

"You're right. Their death had to be avenged."

He exhaled slowly, then ran his hand over the curve of my shoulder and asked, "Why do our conversations keep taking such serious turns?"

"It's just a part of truly getting to know each other. I don't think anyone can ever really understand another person without knowing the bad stuff they lived through. In my case, those events changed me, and they still affect me. It's why I try to be totally self-sufficient, and why I tend to withdraw from the world."

"In what way do you withdraw?"

"I have very few friends, and I've gotten to the point where I barely leave the house," I admitted. "I guess I just feel safest there."

"You must get lonely."

"I did, especially after Griffin got married. It got to the point that I actually tried a dating app, but what I wanted more than anything was just to make a new friend."

"I find myself wanting to beat up every single person you dated," he said. "I'd like to say it's because of the mate bond, but I might actually be that possessive."

"There was only one. Actually, I met him the same night Carter found me. I couldn't even go through with kissing him, and he left after about fifteen minutes." My phone was on the nightstand, and I reached for it as I said, "Now that I'm thinking about it, I really should delete my dating profile."

"Yes you should, but show me first. I'm really curious." Elias grinned at me, and we both sat up a bit.

"Okay, but don't laugh." I accessed the app with a few taps of the screen, and when I handed him the phone, Elias burst out laughing. I chuckled too and asked, "What did I just say?"

"I'm sorry, but this is hilarious. You used a picture of a bulldog for your dating profile."

"Technically, that's a picture of me." He started laughing again, and I grinned and said, "Well, what was I going to do, use a photo of what I look like now? Rule number one when hiding from a fated mate is don't post pictures online."

"That makes sense. Let's see what you wrote here," he said, as he scrolled down. "Matt, age twenty-seven, mechanic. You aren't five-foot-ten."

"I'm also not twenty-seven."

"Can you imagine if you listed your real age?" I chuckled at that as he kept reading. "This doesn't say much. I was hoping for insights into what you're looking for in a man."

"I'm looking for you."

He smiled at me as he returned my phone. "You really weren't, not when you wrote that."

"I was stupid. Here I was, trying to date frogs while hiding from a prince."

"Can I see the guy you decided to meet?"

"Why, still thinking about beating him up?"

"No. I'm just curious."

As I pulled up Logan's profile, I said, "We chatted for a few days, mostly about cars. Then I decided to take a chance and invite him over, because he seemed like a nice guy."

When I showed him the screen, Elias said, "That's a picture of a blue car."

"More specifically, it's a picture of a 1970 Pontiac Firebird Trans Am. That's what I liked about him, we shared a mutual love of '60s and '70s muscle cars."

"Did you ever see what that guy looked like before inviting him over? Or was the car photo all you needed to find him attractive?" His tone was light, teasing.

"We exchanged photos after we'd been chatting a couple of days," I said, as I scrolled through the messages we'd exchanged. "I'll show you what he sent me." When I found the picture, I murmured, "What the hell?"

"What's wrong?"

I stared at the photo of a blue-eyed brunet on my screen. Then I turned to Elias and told him, "This isn't the man I met. So, who the hell was in my house?"

Chapter 11

Elias looked confused. "What are you talking about?"

I turned to him and asked, "Did you send someone else to find me? A scout maybe, since Carter showed up a few hours later?"

"The only person helping Carter look for you was Desiree," Elias told me. "Please start from the beginning and tell me what happened."

"I talked to this guy online for a few days. His name's Logan. We even video chatted at one point, so I know I was talking to the guy in that photo. But that's not the person who came to my house. For some reason, I thought it was when I saw him. He even had the blue Trans Am, but he didn't look anything like the man in that picture."

"What did he look like?"

I paused to think about that. "I remember brown eyes and blond hair. The rest is hazy, as if…"

"As if someone put a perception spell on you and made you see what they wanted you to."

I nodded and muttered, "That's so creepy."

Elias got up and reached for his clothes. "Let's go talk to Carter and see if he knows anything about this."

Once we were dressed, we left the bedroom hand-in-hand and headed down the hallway. After a moment, I detected a change in air pressure and asked, "Did you feel that?"

"Yeah. We just passed through some kind of spell."

When we reached the living room moments later, Desiree looked up from her laptop and said, "I put a sound-proof dome around you two, so we all didn't have to listen to you fucking. Did you forget most of us have exceptional hearing? I don't know what Elias was doing to you, but damn. Daddy got some skills." She ran her gaze up and down my mate, and he fidgeted self-consciously.

"Thanks for sound-proofing us," I mumbled.

"You're welcome. Your friends are here, by the way. They arrived about fifteen minutes ago, but I figured you were still recovering from all that D, so I told them to let you rest. Everyone's out on the patio, pretending like it's not fucking freezing. I'm the only one with sense, so I'm staying in here." She picked up a wine glass, toasted us, and took a drink before returning her attention to the laptop.

We went outside through a sliding glass door, and Griffin looked up from a tablet and called, "Hey, Matty!" His beautiful husband Ari was sitting on his lap, and he smiled at me and waved before turning a curious gaze to Elias.

Griffin turned back to the screen and spewed baby talk for a few moments before saying, "Bye for now, Newty-Newt. We love you!"

Elias whispered, "Newty-Newt?"

"A nickname for Newton, his puppy."

Griffin was saying, "Thanks again for dog-sitting for us, Aunt Lil. We'll talk to you soon."

Meanwhile, Elias asked, "Does he really call you Matty?"

"Yes, but I'm trying to break him of the habit. At least he finally stopped calling me Fig."

"Why did he call you a piece of fruit?"

"It was my name when I was—"

"His bulldog?"

Elias looked amused, and I sighed and said, "Yes. That."

"But why Fig?"

"It was taken from my last name, Figueroa. Fig was his mom's nickname for me. We were friends. I can't remember if I already told you that."

Elias grinned and asked, "Did Griffin use baby talk with you, like he just did with the puppy?"

I chuckled and poked his ribs as my friends got up and crossed the patio to us. Ari reached us first and gave me a big hug. Then Griffin put his arm around my shoulders, led me away from Elias, and pressed a hand to my forehead. When I asked what he was doing, he said, "Checking to see if you're bespelled."

"Why would I be?"

"Because all of a sudden, you're very cozy with the man you hated for a century," he said. "Carter swears you aren't, but maybe Reyes got someone else to do it."

I hugged my friend and said, "I'm fine, and I was wrong about Elias. He's absolutely wonderful, and I don't know if I'll ever forgive myself for missing out on the last century with him."

Griffin brushed his dark hair from his eyes as he told me, "This is a total one-eighty from where you were the last time we saw each other. You know that, right?"

"I know." I took my friend's hand and smiled at him. "Come and meet him. I think you'll be pleasantly surprised."

He let me guide him back across the patio, and I said, "Griffin Vale and Ari Bloom, I'd like you to meet my mate, Elias Reyes."

Elias stuck his hand out and said, "Mateo speaks very highly of you."

Griffin gripped his hand firmly as he narrowed his dark eyes and studied him closely. Next, sweet, lovely Ari, the former angel, gave Elias a hug and said, "Welcome to the family."

His husband sighed and asked, "Isn't that a bit premature, babe?"

"I can feel the current between them," Ari said, as he tucked a blond curl behind his ear. "That's not just their mate bond. They genuinely care about each other."

I wrapped my hands around Elias's arm and said, "I could have told you that." Then I turned my attention to Carter, who'd been deep in conversation with August and Tinder on the edge of the patio. As he got up to refill his wine glass, I asked him, "On Friday night, did you send a scout to my house before you found me?"

"No. Why do you ask?"

I told him about the imposter who'd showed up for my date, and how I'd been bespelled into thinking it was someone else. Then I asked, "Do you think the brothers could have been behind that?"

"I wouldn't put it past them," he said.

"Why didn't they take me prisoner?"

"Because they didn't want you, they wanted Elias. They must have found out I was searching for his mate and tracked you down before I did. Then they made sure I'd find you, with a trail leading directly from those fireworks." Carter shook his head and muttered, "They really weren't subtle, were they? And I played right into their hands by bringing you to the island. No wonder they found him in Maine."

I shivered a little and said, "I wonder who they sent to my house."

Carter shrugged. "They have a lot of people working for them, so it could have been anyone."

"If that's really what happened, then they know where you live," Tinder said, as he and August joined us. "That means you can't go home, Mateo, not until we deal with the brothers once and for all."

I turned to Griffin and Ari and asked, "Did they already tell you about the brothers?"

"Yeah, two super-powerful demons with more fire power than all of us combined. That sucks." Griffin knit his brows and said, "You know what I just realized? I sent Tinder and August to the house to check on you. If the brothers are monitoring that location, how long will it be before they track them to this place?"

The vampires glanced at each other, and August said, "We should relocate, just to be on the safe side. I'm going to pack a few things. Let's all be ready to go in five minutes. I'll let Desiree know what we're doing."

Tinder followed him inside, and I turned to Elias. He read the worry in my eyes and wrapped his arms around me as he said, "I'm so sorry for bringing this down on you and your friends."

I stretched up to kiss him before saying, "It's not your fault."

A few minutes later, we all gathered in the garage, and August said, "We'll take my brother Laurence's SUV, because it's big enough to hold all of us. He and his partner are out of the country, so they won't miss it. Tinder and Mateo's cars both stand out, so we should keep them hidden for now."

Desiree said, "I need to borrow a car. I'm heading back to L.A., so I can monitor what the brothers are up to."

Carter asked, "Are you sure it's safe?"

"Of course. My entire network is underground, and if there's one thing I've learned to do over the last three hundred years, it's fly under the radar." She shot us a look and added, "I know what you're thinking, and you're right. I look damn good for three hundred."

Carter turned to us and said, "I'm not sure if I should stay with you or return to L.A. I'm pretty confident the new spells I cast will keep me hidden from the brothers, though I was wrong about that once, and they managed to track me all the way to the east coast."

"It's up to you," Elias said, "but I'd feel better if you were with us. If they do track us down somehow, you'll be able to defend us. Assuming both brothers don't come for us at once."

"Then it's decided. I'll come with you." Carter and Desiree said their goodbyes, and August handed her the keys to a black Range Rover. She gave us a single nod before speeding off into the night.

I turned to Griffin and Ari and said, "You two would probably be safer on your own. The brothers think you're in France, because that's what I told whoever came to the house. It would be best not to attract their attention."

Ari shook his head and told me, "We're all going to stick together." That was the end of the discussion, as far as he and his husband were concerned.

Griffin moved their luggage to the back of the SUV and pulled their car into the garage, and we all climbed into the huge Mercedes-Benz. August slid behind the wheel with Tinder riding shotgun and started the engine. Once he rolled out of the garage, the doors closed behind us, and a faint flash of light told me their wards had engaged.

When we reached the coast highway, August headed north. As we settled in, Carter chatted with Griffin and Ari in the middle row of seats, and Elias and I curled up together in the third row.

After a while, I took my phone from my pocket and sent a text. When I frowned at the reply I got a minute later, Elias asked, "What's wrong?"

"I messaged Logan—the real one—to ask what happened on Friday night. He had no idea who I was or what I was talking about. That must mean the imposter intercepted him and wiped his memory before he could show up for our date, then took his place."

Griffin muttered, "That's really sinister."

"It is. I wonder if I'll ever know who he was. He even tried to kiss me at one point, and I'm so fucking glad I didn't let him." I paused for a few moments, playing the evening back in my mind before saying, "It's eerie that I remember our entire date, but his face just won't come into focus."

"I'm just so grateful he didn't hurt you, whoever he was," Elias said, as he wrapped his arms around me.

Six hours later, we reached August and Tinder's vacation home on California's central coast. I climbed out of the SUV and asked, "Are you sure we'll be safe here?"

August went around to the back of the Mercedes and took out a suitcase as he said, "There's no paper trail connecting Tinder or me to this house, and very few people know it exists. Even if they figure out who we are, the brothers won't be able to link us to this place. Also, I feel it's much safer than a hotel, because it's totally private. The nearest neighbors are miles away."

Carter told us, "I'm going to beef up the wards, just to be on the safe side," and left the garage.

The house was situated at the edge of a cliff above the Pacific, surrounded by forest on three sides. It was an elegant composition of wood and glass, designed to blend into its surroundings. Although it was beautiful, it was also on the small side, and it would probably be cramped with seven of us hiding out here.

As everyone grabbed their luggage and started to head inside, I told my friends, "We'll be in soon. I want to stretch my legs for a few minutes."

I took Elias's hand and led him down a path that followed the cliff's edge. "I don't think we're going to have much privacy in that house, so I wanted to steal you away for a few minutes," I told him, once I figured we were out of earshot. "I hope that's okay."

"It's exactly what I wanted."

It was late and the moon was full, casting its sparkling reflection across the endless expanse of ocean. It stirred up a feeling of restlessness in me, and it seemed to have the same effect on Elias. We walked in silence for a while, until he said, "I'm a little jealous of your vampire friends."

"Why?"

"Since vampires are made, not born, they're the only nonhuman species on earth that still exists in its true, undiluted form. The rest of us have to live our lives as fragments of what we might have been. On nights like this, the pull of the moon is so strong. It stirs up all kinds of feelings, and this intense longing. But I'll never know what it's like to shift into my wolf form and run wild."

"I know exactly what you mean. But even if we can't shift, we can still run wild." I flashed him a smile, then took off at a sprint, yelling, "I'll bet you can't catch me!" He burst out laughing and ran after me.

We dashed through the moonlit forest, weaving among the trees, leaping over rocks, ducking under branches. Both of us were so fast that the woods flew by in a blur. I had a feeling he could catch me any time he wanted to, but we both let it go on for a while because it was exhilarating.

Finally, when I was halfway across a clearing, Elias swept me off my feet and into his arms as I laughed delightedly. He slowed to a jog, then dropped to the ground and claimed me with a fiery kiss, which was laced with a growl.

I grinned as he pinned me beneath him and licked my neck. He got up a few moments later and pulled me to my feet, but I playfully pushed him into a seated position on a nearby boulder.

Then I dropped to my knees in front of him, unzipped his jeans, and pulled down the front of his briefs, exposing his cock. I licked the tip and sucked it almost experimentally, which elicited a soft moan. When it swelled between my lips, that gave me the confidence to continue.

Since I was so inexperienced, I paid close attention and let his sounds guide me. There was something deeply satisfying about pleasuring him like this, such a direct connection between what I was doing and how he responded. I tried different things, licking, sucking, and caressing his cock and balls as I drove him toward his climax.

Just a few minutes later, my efforts paid off. His yell was primal, and he fucked my mouth as he shot down my throat. I moaned with pleasure around his thick shaft and kept sucking until he was spent.

He was gasping for breath when he finished, and he leaned back and propped himself up with both hands on the boulder. Meanwhile, I tucked him in and zipped him up again before climbing onto his lap.

Once he caught his breath, he kissed me and murmured, "You're amazing." That made me smile.

He picked me up and started carrying me through the woods, so I wrapped my arms and legs around him and rested my head on his shoulder. After a while, I asked, "Do you think we'll be safe here?"

"We should be. Our best bet is to keep moving every few days, but I think we'll be okay here for now." He held me a little tighter, and after a few moments he said, "I know that's no way to live, and it won't be forever. This is just until we come up with a plan and figure out how to defeat the brothers once and for all." I wasn't sure a plan like that could be found, but I nodded anyway.

After another minute, the house came into view. It was lit up from within and looked warm and inviting. When we went inside, we found the two couples in the living room, chatting over drinks while a fire crackled in the river rock fireplace. The furniture was comfortable and understated in warm earth tones, and as I settled onto a loveseat, Elias asked, "Where's Carter?"

"He's in his room. There are only three bedrooms, so he took the den," August told us.

Elias said, "I'm going to go check on him," and after August pointed him in the right direction, he left the living room.

Tinder was leaning against his husband with one of his legs draped over August's thigh, and he asked me, "We've busted out the bourbon. Want some?"

When I nodded, he poured me the equivalent of three shots and handed me a glass. "Thank you, not just for the drink," I said. "I really appreciate all you're doing to help us." I turned to Griffin and Ari, who were curled up together on a fluffy area rug in front of the hearth, and added, "I'm so grateful to you two as well. I still can't believe you cut your honeymoon short, just because you thought I was in trouble."

"We're family," Griffin said, "and family looks out for each other."

I muttered, "I just hate the fact that helping us means putting all of your lives in danger."

"Keeping you and Elias alive is obviously the top priority for all of us, but don't forget there's a bigger picture here," August said. "The brothers need to be stopped, no question."

"If we can draw them out and separate them, we have a real shot at taking them down," Tinder added, "and you two are the perfect bait." He said that with a cheerful smile, and he actually had a point.

Carter and Elias joined us a few moments later. My mate settled in right beside me on the loveseat, and Carter took a club chair on the other side of the coffee table. As he poured bourbon into two more glasses, August said, "Apologies for not having anything to eat here. We'll rectify that in the morning when the shops are open."

I had to ask, because I didn't really know Griffin's friends all that well. "Will you two need to…hunt, I guess? I'm not sure how you feed yourselves."

August looked amused. "We'll stop off at a local blood bank tomorrow and compel a nice, cooperative human into giving us a supply."

"Hunting is way more trouble than it's worth. Also, in case you're wondering, werewolves are never on the menu. Too gamey," Tinder said with a grin. I had no idea if he was kidding. Then he changed the subject with, "This has been a long, stressful day, and I think we should hold off on making plans and discussing strategy until tomorrow morning. So, does anybody feel like watching a movie? That's always been my go-to when I need to unwind."

When we agreed, he got up and opened a cabinet to reveal a TV, then rifled through a drawer of Blu-ray discs and made a decision for us. As *Alien* began to play, Elias and I shifted around a bit so I was leaning against him, and he wrapped his arms around me.

The movie turned out to be a great distraction. For two hours, we all got to pretend we were perfectly normal people leading perfectly normal lives. Tinder had seen the movie about a million times and kept whispering key lines, then making us all jump by doing his version of a cat scare a split-second before every scary part. It would have been annoying if it wasn't so funny.

Later that night, Elias and I returned to our room and curled up naked in that warm, comfortable bed, which was bathed in moonlight. Then we spent hours alternately kissing and talking quietly about whatever came to mind. In the hour before dawn, he traced my lower lip with his fingertip and said, "You should try to get some sleep."

"I'm not sure I can. There's too much on my mind."

He pulled the blanket up and shifted around so my back was pressed to his chest. It surprised me when he began to sing. The song was in Spanish, and I didn't know the name of it, but it was so gentle and soothing that it seemed like a lullaby.

When he finished, I took his hand and hugged it to my chest as I whispered, "No one's ever sung to me before."

"Did you like it?"

"I loved it."

"Then I promise to sing for you any time you want me to."

After a while, I whispered, "I'm so scared about what's going to happen if and when the brothers find us."

"I know I'm the only person in our group without any magical ability," he said, "but I promise I'll protect you, Mateo. I'll do whatever it takes to keep you safe." I really believed he would.

Chapter 12

The next day dawned with blue skies, a rarity on the central coast this time of year. Griffin went out and bought some groceries, and Elias and I joined the newlyweds for breakfast. We tried to keep the conversation light, and they told us about all they'd seen and done in Paris. But there was an undercurrent of worry, and we all felt it.

Meanwhile, Carter was pacing outside. He kept checking his phone every few minutes, and once we finished eating, I joined him and asked, "Anything wrong?"

"I'm not sure. Early this morning, some kind of power surge took out every camera we had set up around the compound. Desiree sent some people to do surveillance, but for about twenty minutes, no one had eyes on that place. I hate not knowing for a fact whether the brothers are still inside."

I took his hand, which was cold to the touch, and said, "Come have some coffee. Even if the sun's shining, it's freezing out here." He met my gaze with concern in his pale gray eyes, and I told him, "You can check your phone just as easily from the kitchen."

He let me lead him inside, and I directed him to my seat at the table before bringing him some coffee and a croissant. While he and Elias discussed this latest development, I went and found

August and Tinder. They were playing chess at a small table by a window in the living room, and Tinder was sitting on his husband's lap. Whenever it was Tinder's turn, he barely glanced at the board, then leaned over and made some type of bold move that always seemed to surprise August. When Tinder announced, "Checkmate," August sighed and slumped in his seat, and Tinder grinned at him.

I repeated what Carter had told me, and August said, "That's not great news, but it doesn't necessarily mean they've left the compound, or that they know where to find us."

"That's true. Just to be on the safe side though, is there anything we can do to prepare ourselves? I feel so helpless just sitting here and waiting to see if something will happen."

"Tyler and I already spent the morning searching my library," August said. "I have texts spanning several centuries on a range of paranormal subjects, which have all been scanned and stored digitally. There was no information to be found on how to defeat a demon, let alone two."

I returned to the kitchen and asked Carter, "How long has it been since Desiree's cameras were knocked out?"

He glanced at his watch. "Almost three hours."

"It's only, what, an hour to fly here from L.A.?"

"About that," Carter said.

"Just because the cameras were knocked out doesn't mean the brothers are on their way here," Elias told me. He had a point, but I just couldn't shake the feeling that something was wrong.

He tried to distract me by leading me to the other end of the kitchen and showing me how to make bread. He'd sent a shopping list with Griffin that morning and planned to make lunch for all of us. Well, those of us who weren't vampires, anyway.

The process of breadmaking was surprisingly soothing. He talked me through the steps, demonstrating techniques when needed, and for a little while I forgot about everything but the soft, pliable dough in my hands.

We'd just finished kneading it and transferred it to a bowl to rise when the hair on the back of my neck prickled. A moment later, a slight tremor shook the house. I whispered, "They found us," as fear shot through me.

Everyone ran into the kitchen, and Griffin said, "Please tell me that was just an earthquake."

I reached out with my senses and shook my head. "There are two demons just outside the wards, along with eight…no, ten vampires." I tried to get a sense of what they were doing and muttered, "I think they brought the vampires for the entertainment value. They plan to have them attack us first, because it'd be over too quickly if the brothers fought us head-on."

Tinder startled us by smashing one of his wooden kitchen chairs against the floor. Then he picked up two of the jagged, broken legs and tossed one to August as he said, "Bring it on." His eyes glimmered with excitement, and he actually grinned.

Another tremor shook the house. There was nowhere to run or hide, so I said, "I want to see who we're up against," and headed to the front door.

So far, the wards were holding them back. I had to wonder, though—were they just toying with us? It seemed a bit like jailers rattling their prisoners' cell doors just to mess with them.

The seven of us stepped out the front door and squared our shoulders as we stared down our enemies. Ten newly made vampires were pacing and growling, totally bloodthirsty and inhuman. Beyond them stood two tall figures dressed in black—the brothers. Cain, the white-haired man I'd glimpsed when we were speeding away from the compound, smiled at me. It sent a shiver down my spine.

Abel had a slim build, unruly, golden-blond hair, and dark eyes. I whispered, "Oh god," as I met his gaze. Then I told Elias, "That's the man who came to my house and pretended to be Logan."

Anger welled in me. I stepped forward, stopping a few feet from the invisible barrier, and yelled to Abel, "How did you find me?"

He answered me by letting his memories play through my mind. I saw him meeting an informant, someone Elias had hired in the past to search for me, who gave him a sketch of what I looked like. That sketch was then distributed throughout Southern California, by hundreds of people brainwashed to help the brothers. In just a matter of days, someone spotted me at the liquor store, so they staked it out and discovered I showed up there most Friday nights.

Abel himself was waiting for me in the parking lot the night I went to buy the wine, hidden behind an invisibility spell. He read my thoughts and decided to intercept my date and take his place, just because that seemed like fun to him. He followed me home, waited at the foot of my driveway for the real Logan, then bespelled him and read his mind. Abel left him standing on the side of the road while he took his car. Then he cast another spell to assume Logan's identity and make sure I only read him as a warlock, not a demon. The plan was to find a way to lead Carter to my house, because they'd learned he was looking for me, and they knew he'd take me right to Elias.

A sick feeling twisted my gut when I saw how he'd tracked us to the island, then to this house. During our "date" Abel had planted a kind of psychic gateway in my brain, so he could monitor my thoughts and, to some extent, see through my eyes. It wasn't fool-proof, and the concealment spell I'd cast on myself before I left for the compound made it cut in and out. But it had given Abel enough information to be able to piece it together and find us here.

I felt his smug satisfaction and wanted to punch him in the face. Not only was he proud of himself, this was all just a big game to him. Tracking me down had been fun, the way someone might work a puzzle.

"I feel sorry for you," I yelled, across the twenty feet that separated us. "You've spent all of eternity never caring about anyone but yourself. Now you live among humans, but you don't understand them. You don't understand anything—not love or compassion, happiness or sadness. You like to pretend you're better than us, but being stronger doesn't make you better. It just makes you a bully, a thing to be hated and feared."

He locked eyes with me, rage building in him as I continued, "Actually, you're not even that. You're just Cain's puppet. His errand boy. He sent you to fetch Elias in Maine because he couldn't be bothered, right? That's why the task of finding me fell to you, too, because it was beneath your other half. Your *better* half. Cain calls all the shots, doesn't he? And for millennia, you've always just done what you're told, too much of a fucking lap dog to think for yourself!"

A low growl rumbled in Abel's throat, and he raised a hand. The ground began to shake so violently that my friends and I fell to our knees, and Tinder called, "Um, maybe stop poking the bear, Mateo."

"What difference does it make? He's going to kill us anyway," I said, as I stood up again and met Abel's gaze. "We don't stand a chance against two demons, and they know it. As soon as these wards fall, their vampire pets are going to try their damnedest to rip us to shreds, which will be so fucking amusing, won't it, Abel? Then when they're good and ready, the brothers will finish us off."

I lowered my voice, my eyes still locked with Abel's, and said, "People call you the brothers, Cain and Abel. But you know how that story ends, right? Spoiler alert, Cain kills Abel. After you've burned this world to the ground and there's no other way for him to amuse himself, how long will it be before he turns on you, Abel? How long before making you suffer becomes his entertainment?"

Cain's yell was terrifying and utterly inhuman. He raised his hands and wrenched them in opposite directions, and the air between us lit up in blue as the wards tore in half, then rained down like shards of glass before disappearing.

The moment the barrier broke, the vampires descended on us. I threw one aside with a wave of my arm, then held out my hands and conjured an energy shield to try to deflect anything the brothers threw at us.

Griffin rushed forward, thrust his hands out, and threw two vampires a hundred feet back with a burst of energy. At the same time, Elias grabbed a thick fallen branch and snapped it in two, then stood at my side with his makeshift stakes, brave and determined. When a vampire rushed at us, my mate spun around and struck him in the chest. The creature was reduced to dust as his clothes drifted to the ground.

Meanwhile, August and Tinder fought in perfect unison. Tinder staked one of the vampires, then rolled out of the way as another lunged at him. August finished that one off by driving his stake through him, and then he pulled his husband to his feet. The two men stood back-to-back, powerful and united, then took out two more vampires with the grace of a choreographed dance.

While the brothers were distracted by the mayhem they'd unleashed, Griffin gathered all the energy he could muster and fired it at Cain. For just a moment, the demon was knocked on his ass. But then he rose up, looking fierce and otherworldly, and flicked his wrist. The force obliterated my shield and sent Griffin slamming into the front of the house, hard enough to crack the wall.

Ari was by his side in an instant. Griffin had been knocked unconscious, and I shouted to his husband, "Get him out of here!"

Tiny, delicate Ari scooped his husband into his arms, and then he stood up, bold and fearless. White light shot from him as a pair of pristine, white wings unfurled behind him. The brothers hesitated, startled to suddenly discover an angel in their midst. If only Ari still had his powers.

Since he didn't, he did the only thing he could—he saved his husband. Ari raised his wings, then brought them down so forcefully that Elias and I had to brace ourselves against the sudden gust of wind. He shot straight up into the air, then darted away so quickly that he and Griffin disappeared from sight in an instant.

Carter used that temporary distraction to attack Cain. Black lightning shot from his hands, crackling and humming with power. His eyes went black and looked like they were lit from within as he gritted his teeth. Cain staggered back. But then he straightened up again and turned an equally powerful force on Carter, sparks flying twenty feet into the air when the second stream of black lightning collided with the first.

Abel turned his attention to Elias and me, and I quickly pulled up the shield again. I felt him gathering his power before I saw it. He formed a glowing ball of dark energy between his hands, turning it over and over as it grew in strength.

My heart was pounding in my ears. I put everything I had into that shield and just prayed it would hold. Abel drew his arm back, and I held my breath.

Then he threw it, and the ball of energy tore through my shield like it was made of wet paper. I braced for the impact, sure I wouldn't survive it.

But then, in the split second before it reached us, Elias threw himself in front of me and took the full force of the attack. His face contorted with pain. It seemed as if time slowed down, and I watched in horror as his body bent and twisted from the impact. I grabbed him as he fell to the ground and was pulled down with him.

I felt our mate bond snap, then vanish as Elias died in my arms.

I stared at my mate's lifeless body for a long, terrible moment. Then I screamed and thrust a hand at Abel. As tears poured down my cheeks, I pushed into the demon's mind, using the gateway he'd established to track me. I made him feel everything—my pain, my horror, the overwhelming sense of loss, and exactly what Elias meant to me.

There was nothing left to fight for, but before I died I wanted him to understand exactly what he'd destroyed.

Abel took a step back, and his arms fell to his sides. I kept pushing my emotions into his mind, because I wanted him to hurt like I was hurting. I sobbed uncontrollably, clutching Elias's lifeless body.

The demon took another step back and looked around. He seemed disoriented. Tinder and August were battling the remaining vampires, and Carter and Cain were still locked in their showdown with the streams of energy sparking and crackling between them, but Carter was starting to weaken. When he dropped to one knee, I knew he wouldn't last much longer.

All of a sudden, Abel appeared right before me. He'd moved so fast, I hadn't even registered it.

He knelt down and pressed his hand to Elias's chest. I felt a wave of energy flow through him, and in the next instant, Elias gasped for breath and sat up. Sobs of relief shook me.

I let Abel feel that, too—my elation, my gratitude, all of it. He met my gaze, then reached out and touched the tears streaming down my face, as if he was trying to understand them. I whispered, "Thank you."

His voice was soft when he said, "I'm sorry." He touched my forehead, and I felt a dull ache for just a moment. When he took his hand away, I knew for a fact the connection he'd opened to track me was closed.

"Help us," I begged. "Help Carter, or we're all going to die. Please."

Abel stood up while I gathered Elias into my arms. He took a few steps toward Carter and Cain, just as Tinder and August staked the last of the vampire horde and grabbed each other in an embrace.

Cain glanced at Abel and yelled, "What are you waiting for? Help me finish him, you idiot!"

Abel strode to Carter's side and held out his hand. When Carter took it, Abel pulled him to his feet. Then he kept holding on to it as he turned to Cain and raised his other hand.

The force that hit Cain from Carter and Abel's combined powers felt like a hundred lightning strikes all at once and made the earth vibrate. Cain's yell was furious and terrifying. We shielded ourselves with our hands as a blinding flash of pure white light tore from the demon, and then Cain flew apart in a million shards of light and energy. Everyone was knocked back as a shockwave rolled past us, and then all the windows on the front of the house shattered inward.

Abruptly, the light disappeared. My ears were ringing. It was jarring to suddenly find myself in a perfectly tranquil setting, when moments ago there'd been pure chaos.

It startled me when Ari and Griffin suddenly landed beside me. Griffin looked pale but not much worse for wear, and he stuck his hand out and hauled first me, then Elias to our feet as he said, "We almost missed the good part." Ari's wings seemed to roll in on themselves, and a second later they were gone.

Abel and Carter both stood up, and as Carter brushed some dirt off his suit, Abel looked around at all of us. After a moment, he said, "I need to go and repair some of the damage I've done, assuming you decide to let me live."

Carter glanced at us, and when Elias nodded, he told Abel, "You're free to go." The demon gave a single nod and started to walk away, but Carter called after him, "There's just one more thing."

Abel turned back to him with a curious expression, and Carter closed the gap between them. He pulled Abel into his arms and claimed his mouth in a demanding kiss. Then he let go of him and said, "Until next time."

Abel looked startled. Then he grinned, just a little, before turning and walking down the road. He passed right by the SUVs that must have brought him here, and when he was maybe fifty feet away, a pair of huge, black wings unfurled at his back. He drove them downward and shot into the sky, disappearing from sight in an instant.

I turned to Elias, who looked troubled. He pressed a hand to his chest and asked, "Why can't I feel you?"

"Because mate bonds are severed when one partner dies."

"I don't understand."

"You died saving me," I told him, as I took his face between my hands. "You threw yourself in the way of Abel's attack and shielded me with your body. Don't you remember?"

He thought about it before saying, "I remember searing pain. The next thing I knew, I was in your arms and you were crying."

"Abel brought you back."

"I didn't know demons could do that."

I shrugged and said, "The power we wield is based on electricity, so I suppose he acted as a living defibrillator and restarted your heart. I'm sure a big dose of magic didn't hurt, either."

Since he was a bit shaky, I supported him with an arm around his waist as we headed into the house. He asked, "What made him decide to bring me back to life?"

"A crash course in humanity," I said. "I used a psychic connection he'd established to make Abel feel everything I did when you died. It seemed like empathy was a new concept to him, but he got the idea pretty quickly and brought you back."

"But not our mate bond."

"That was out of his control."

We trudged into the living room, crunching over broken glass, and Elias and I collapsed onto the couch. August and Tinder dropped down next to us, and I glanced at the couple as they leaned against each other. They were smeared with dirt, blood-spattered, and clearly exhausted. Tinder's black T-shirt had been torn almost in half. But they smiled at each other before leaning in for a kiss.

Meanwhile, Carter hovered nearby, and after a moment he said, "I'm going to help myself to one of Abel's abandoned SUVs and head back to L.A. I want to give Desiree an update, and I also want to make sure all the humans in the compound are set free."

I asked, "Don't you want to rest for a few minutes? That had to take a lot out of you."

He adjusted his tie as he said, "I'm fine. I'll check in with you tomorrow." And with that, he took off.

As Griffin and Ari curled up together on the loveseat, Griffin asked, "Do you think it's really over, or did we just make a huge mistake by letting Abel go?"

"He knows he's outgunned," I said. "Any of us plus Carter could take him down. But even without that threat hanging over him, I think I might have gotten through to him today. Abel made the choice to bring Elias back after he killed him, so that tells me there's hope for him."

Griffin's eyes went wide, and he blurted, "Wait, what?"

"Elias died saving my life. He shielded me when Abel blasted us."

Tinder said, "If he died, even just for a minute, that must mean your mate bond is——"

I finished for him. "Gone forever."

He asked, "So, what does that mean for the two of you?"

"It doesn't change a thing," I said, as I snuck a glance at Elias. I could only hope he felt the same way I did.

Chapter 13

That afternoon, Elias and I decided we really wanted to go home, so we said goodbye to our friends and helped ourselves to the second of Abel's abandoned SUVs. We took turns napping during most of the drive back from Big Sur, and the rest of the time we were both pretty quiet. We were both mentally and physically exhausted, and suddenly facing his own mortality had left Elias rattled—understandably so.

On top of that, we were trying to come to grips with our new reality, now that the mate bond was gone forever. One thing was clear—I had very real feelings for Elias, and I could only hope that was mutual. I'd already known the things I felt for him hadn't been because of the bond, but its absence still left me feeling fragmented and insecure. There was a void where the bond had been, and neither of us quite knew how to handle it.

It was obvious now that when Carter had suppressed the bond, he'd failed to suppress all of it. Now that it really was gone, things between us just felt different, unfamiliar, as if the whole world had shifted beneath our feet and we were still struggling to find our balance.

Given that, it meant a lot to me when Elias asked, "Will you stay with me tonight?" I readily agreed.

When we reached August and Tinder's house, we traded the SUV for my Barracuda. Then we continued on to Santa Monica. It was pretty late by the time we reached Elias's upscale neighborhood. The multimillion dollar homes ranged in architectural style from classic to modern, all of them gorgeous and elegant. Elias's house was another thing entirely.

I punched in the code he gave me on a keypad at the foot of the driveway, and as the gate swung open, I decided it was the most unwelcoming house I'd ever seen. It was basically an imposing concrete block that gave off a prison vibe.

When we reached the garage, he jumped out of the car and typed in another code to open the door. I pulled in next to a silver, vintage Jaguar, and the garage door closed behind us. Getting into the house and disarming the alarm required more codes and more keypads. All of that just added to the prison vibe.

Once inside, we made our way down a long hallway past a bunch of closed doors. When we reached the center of the building, I murmured, "Oh wow."

The huge living room was mostly white and sparsely furnished. It reminded me of an art gallery, with several abstract paintings and sculptures on display. "I know this must seem sterile, but please reserve judgement for one more minute," he said.

I followed him across the room to a locked door, which he opened with yet another code and keypad. I had to ask. "What's with all the security?"

"Even before I got on the brothers' bad side, I made plenty of enemies. That's pretty inevitable in my line of work. This place was built to totally lock down if need be, including armored shutters that slide shut over all the windows."

I muttered, "I see," as I followed him down another long hallway.

"Whenever anyone comes over, which isn't often, they only see that living room back there, which I consider the 'public' part of the house. These rooms are private."

He opened another door, and I actually gasped. That's how different it was than the rest of the house. I stepped into a spacious room all done up in warm wood and deep jewel tones, with a grand piano and floor-to-ceiling shelves full of books. "This is more like it," I said, as I perched on the edge of the L-shaped, dark red couch. There was a door in one corner, and I asked, "Where does that lead?"

"The kitchen. Well, one of them. There's a big, modern kitchen in the other wing of the house, but I found I didn't really like it, so I had another one built." He seemed embarrassed as he added, "My bedroom's through there," and gestured at an open doorway to my right. I got up and followed him into the master suite.

It, too, was warm and welcoming, decorated in that same rich color palette. The focal point of the room was a huge bed made up with deep sapphire linens, and directly across from the bed was a fireplace with a portrait above it—of me. The oil painting looked like the work of a Renaissance master, right down to the softly draped, white silk shirt, which was unbuttoned and dipped seductively off one shoulder. Now I understood why he seemed embarrassed.

I grinned and said, "I look like I'm ready for the cover of a regency romance novel."

He muttered, "I'm mortified. What must you think of me?"

"That you're a man who cared deeply for his mate. Did you paint that?" When he nodded, I said, "It's an excellent likeness."

Elias seemed a bit lost when he turned to me. "This must all seem strange, and more than a little eccentric. I've been on my own for a very long time, and I designed a home to suit my far from conventional life."

"I totally understand."

An awkward silence stretched between us. Finally, he asked, "Are you hungry?"

"No. Just tired."

He nodded and found me a new toothbrush, and I stepped into the pristine, dark blue master bathroom. When I emerged a few minutes later, dressed for bed in my T-shirt and briefs, he slipped past me to take a turn getting ready for bed.

I stood in the center of the bedroom while I waited for him to return, shifting my weight from one foot to the other, and eyed my portrait. He'd either misremembered or taken some liberties with my hair, which was thick, wavy, and shoulder-length, and made me look a bit like a Latin Fabio. Then again, maybe the original Fabio was already Latin. I actually had no idea.

I paced around a bit before opening the doors to the balcony. There was a sweeping ocean view, and the breeze was cold, but I left the doors open anyway and breathed deeply.

I was both weary and disoriented. I'd totally lost track of what day of the week it was. Had it really only been the night before that Elias and I walked along the cliffs and ran through the forest? The moon was still full, and that was still the Pacific, but our night in Big Sur felt like it had happened a lifetime ago.

By the time Elias returned to the bedroom dressed in a T-shirt and black pajama pants, I was shivering. He turned on the gas fireplace with the flip of a switch while I shut the balcony doors, and then I joined him under the covers.

As he plugged in a phone on the nightstand, he told me, "Carter sent a message to tell us the compound is totally abandoned. Desiree said Abel returned and set all the humans free before firing his staff and driving away. He left all the doors and gates open. Desiree says if he doesn't return, she's going to take it over and turn it into her version of Hogwarts."

"I can totally see her doing that."

He turned off the lights from a panel by his nightstand, and we stretched out on our sides facing each other with about two feet of mattress between us. After a while, I murmured, "Hell of a day."

"I'm still trying to come to grips with the fact that I literally died."

"Are you okay?"

He shrugged. "I don't think I have demonic energy flowing through me and am about to turn evil or anything."

"I know," I said, "but do you feel alright?"

"I'm fine, just tired. But I think I'm going to be processing this day for a while."

"No doubt." After a pause, I said, "You know what surprised me today?"

"All of it?"

"Well, yes. But I mean the fact that Cain gave off pure white light when he was destroyed. For a second, it looked just like Ari does when he transforms into an angel."

"That's because demons and angels are the same thing deep down, but demons became twisted and corrupted at some point in their history. Not irredeemably, as Carter demonstrates every day."

"And Abel," I said. "He chose the side of good today."

"I hate to think what would have happened if you hadn't gotten through to him. But there's no way of knowing if that's a true change, or just a momentary lapse. Time will tell, I suppose. At least Carter can keep him in check if need be."

I grinned and asked, "What was that kiss about?"

Elias grinned, too. "I'm not sure. Carter doesn't discuss his love life with me, but if he's interested in Abel, he's going to have his hands full."

"No doubt."

We both fell silent again, watching each other in the flickering firelight. Then I reached out and took his hand. He wrapped both of his hands around mine and said, "We're going to be okay, Mateo." I wanted to believe that more than anything.

The next morning, I awoke alone in that big bed. The first thing I noticed was that my portrait no longer hung above the mantel, and in its place was an impressionistic landscape. I tried not to read too much into that, but it still felt a bit like a rejection.

I climbed out of bed and went into the bathroom. Elias had thoughtfully left some things for me on the counter, including a razor and a comb. After I showered and shaved, I got dressed in the same clothes from the day before, because they were all I had with me.

Then I went in search of Elias. A feeling of uncertainty followed me. It was such an odd feeling, not really knowing what we were to each other anymore.

The door in the corner was open when I stepped into the sitting room, and I could hear Elias moving around in the kitchen. I crossed the room, then paused and leaned against the doorframe.

It was tough to sneak up on a werewolf, but I'd managed it because he was lost in thought. He stood at a work table in the center of the small, simple kitchen, barefoot and dressed in a black T-shirt and jeans. The muscles flexed in his arms and shoulders as he kneaded a soft dough, transforming it from a mixture of ingredients into something more.

Without warning, a sense of loss slammed into me.

He was free of the bond now. Free of me. He could find whoever he wanted, fall in love, and build a life with the man of his choice.

Regret rose up and swallowed me whole.

I'd made such a huge mistake and wasted so many years, all because of fear. That was the real thing that had kept me away from him—fear of trusting someone, fear of putting myself in a position where I could be hurt. That was why I ran and hid from him, and that fear had cost me everything. It cost me a century with my mate, and now I didn't have one anymore.

Just then, Elias looked up and spotted me in the doorway. I held my breath, waiting to see what he'd do.

Then the most beautiful smile spread across his face. He was happy to see me. I felt it as well as saw it, that happiness rolling off him in waves.

When I rushed to him, he held his arms out and caught me in an embrace. I clung to him and buried my face in his chest, and he chuckled and said, "I'm getting flour all over you." I just held on tighter, and he asked, very gently, "Are you alright?"

I blurted, "I'm so sorry, Eli."

"What are you apologizing for?"

"Hiding from you. Hurting you. God, I'm sorry."

"That's all in the past."

"But I wasted all those years we could have had together, and now we're not mates anymore, and—"

He tilted my chin up and kissed me tenderly. Then he said, "It doesn't matter if the mate bond is gone. Nothing's changed, Mateo."

"It hasn't?"

"Not for me. Has it changed for you?" When I shook my head, he smiled at me and said, "In that case, we have centuries ahead of us, and they're so full of possibility. That's what we should be focused on, not the past, or things that are out of our control."

I searched his eyes and asked, "Am I really what you want, even without the bond? Even though you can have anyone you choose now?"

"I choose you, Mateo. It's always been you. Don't you know that?"

"But you didn't have a say in it. The universe just randomly put us together, and—"

"No, it didn't. It created the perfect partner for each of us, and then it allowed us to find each other. With or without the bond, you're still my other half, and I'm so grateful for you."

I hugged him tightly and murmured, "I thought I lost you twice in the last twenty-four hours, first when you died, then again when I realized our bond was gone."

He kissed my forehead and said, "You're not getting rid of me that easily."

I grinned at him, then gestured at what he'd been kneading and asked, "Is that going to be breakfast?"

He moved the dough into a big, ceramic bowl and covered it with a blue dish towel, then moved it to the counter as he said, "No, that still has a few hours to go. I baked some brioche for breakfast."

"You must have been up for hours."

He wiped his hands on another dish towel as he said, "I woke up at dawn and couldn't get back to sleep. I've had a lot on my mind."

"Like what?"

"Like where we're going to live, and what I'm going to do now that I'm retiring from my current line of work."

"Wouldn't we live here?" Just then, I noticed my portrait in its new home on the kitchen wall, right where he'd see it as he was working, and exclaimed, "I thought you got rid of that!"

"No. I just moved it out of the bedroom, because I thought you'd find it awkward to wake up to it," he said. "As for your first question, you shouldn't have to live in a fortress, or a place designed to suit only me. We need to either find or build a home for the two of us."

"I'd love that."

"Good. Then we'll start looking right away."

I leaned against the work table and took his hand. "Are you really retiring?"

He nodded. "It's inevitable to make enemies, given what I do, but it's not just about me anymore. It's about us, and I don't want my bad decisions to affect you." He kissed my forehead, and then he gestured in the general direction of the refrigerator and asked, "Are you hungry? I should get breakfast started."

"Not yet. There's something we need to do first." I tried to look very serious as I said that.

"What do we need to do?"

"We need to fuck, right here, right now."

Elias chuckled at that as he picked me up and sat me on the edge of the work table. I pulled him to me and kissed him as he cupped my ass with both hands, and then he climbed up on the table with me and pushed me onto my back.

We ended up getting naked and rolling around in the flour that was left on the work surface. It coated out bodies in a gossamer layer, and my hands slid over the slickness of his skin as he playfully nipped my lower lip.

When I flipped us over so I was on top, a cloud of flour rose into the air, which made us laugh. I ran my fingers over his cheek, leaving white streaks, then leaned down and kissed him again. As I rubbed my stiff cock against his, he murmured, "We really need to buy some lube."

"You're right about that. In the meantime, let's improvise. Again."

We tumbled off the table, and after he found some vegetable oil, I pulled him onto the wood floor with me. He used the oil to finger me open while I poured some into my palm and stroked his thick shaft.

Once we were ready, I straddled his hips and lowered myself onto his hard cock. It was exhilarating to be the one in charge, setting the pace as I pinned his hands down on either side of his head.

I rode him hard and fast, and after a few minutes, he arched off the floor and came in me, throwing his head back and moaning as he thrust deep into my ass. It was so satisfying to see him like this, totally given over to pleasure.

As soon as he finished, he flipped me onto my back and sucked my cock like a man on a mission. It felt incredible, and I totally let go, riding along on pure sensation until I finally shot down his throat. Afterwards, I grinned and ran a hand over his floury chest as I murmured, "We made a mess."

"Easily remedied."

He got up and scooped me into his arms, and when he stepped outside through the kitchen door, I chuckled and told him, "Okay, not what I was expecting." He carried me through an opening in a vine-covered wall, and I murmured, "Oh wow."

He'd brought me to an outdoor shower which was totally ringed with plants, including the half-wall which gave way to a sweeping view of the Pacific. After he adjusted the water so it was nice and warm, we took turns washing each other. Then we wrapped up in towels, and he led me to the pool deck.

There was a throw blanket on the back of the lone lounge chair, and he bundled us up with me on his lap. "This is so nice," I murmured, as I put my head on his shoulder.

"I know you'll want to stay in Southern California because your friends mean a lot to you, but what do you think about finding a home up the coast, somewhere less crowded than L.A.? I'd love to live someplace off by ourselves, where we have some land and lots of privacy."

"That sounds perfect. We'd be able to run wild whenever we wanted to."

"Exactly." As I traced his collarbone, he said, "Do you know how many times I sat out on this deck and imagined you here with me, just like this?" When I started to apologize again for all the years I resisted our bond, he silenced me with a kiss. Then he said, "I'm not saying that to make you feel guilty. I just wanted to let you know I'm very grateful and happy right now. Happier than I've ever been."

"Me, too."

We both watched the sea and the sky for a while, and then he asked, "Would you be willing to travel with me? There's so much I want to show you."

"Where would we go?"

"Central America, maybe? There are some beautiful spots I know of, totally wild and unspoiled. We could make love under a waterfall, and sleep under the stars."

"I haven't traveled in years, but that sounds heavenly."

"Yeah? You think you'd be up for it?"

I nodded. "It's time to get back out there and remember what it means to be alive, instead of just existing. I let my world get very narrow, but with you by my side, I feel like I can take on anything."

He tilted my chin up with a light touch and kissed me. Then, as he traced my jawline, he told me, "I love you so much, Mateo."

"I love you, too."

He looked away, suddenly vulnerable, and murmured, "You don't have to say that, just because I did."

Now it was my turn to tilt his face toward mine with a gentle hand on his cheek. He met my gaze, and as the ocean breeze stirred his hair, I whispered, "I said that because it's the absolute truth. I love you, Elias. You're the best thing that ever happened to me, my perfect other half."

His smile was glorious. He held me close, and for the rest of the morning, we talked excitedly and made plans for our future.

Epilogue

Five Months Later
West Coast of Costa Rica
Central America

"You're never coming home, are you?"

Griffin grinned at me from my phone's screen, and I told him, "Of course we are. Eventually. Our home won't be done for another two months anyway, so there's no hurry."

"Speaking of which, Ari and I just went by the construction site, and your house looks incredible."

"That's good to hear. The architect keeps sending us photos, and it seems to be exactly what Eli and I envisioned."

After we'd decided to build a place to suit both of us, Elias and I had spent a few weeks designing our dream home, which evolved into a beautiful, Mediterranean-style villa that was under construction in the hills north of Malibu. It was very private and surrounded by several acres of land, so we could run wild any time we wanted to.

"It definitely looks like the drawings you showed us," Griffin said.

I asked, "Are you visiting August and Tinder?"

"Yup. Ari's just pulling into their driveway." He tilted the phone toward his husband, who waved at the screen before turning his attention to parking the car. "August's brother and brother-in-law just got back from Europe, and our friends Nate and Nikolai are joining us for a—well, not a dinner party, since they're all vampires. But a get-together, anyway. It's nice that your new home is less than half an hour from August and Tinder's place, by the way. It'll make it easy to visit, if you ever return from Central America."

I smiled at my friend. "Like I said, we'll come back eventually. But just take a look at this place, and you'll see why we're in no hurry to leave." I panned the phone around to show him the white sand beach on the edge of a lush, green jungle.

Up ahead, Elias and a man in a Hawaiian shirt were waiting for me outside a tiny, emerald green chapel, and Griffin said, "Hang on. Why are you and Eli dressed up?"

We were both wearing white, button-down shirts and tan linen pants, and I grinned at my friend and said, "This isn't exactly dressed up, but we thought we should get married in something nicer than T-shirts and shorts."

Griffin yelled, "Holy shit, Matty! Why didn't you tell me you're getting married?"

"I'm telling you now," I said with a smile. "Will you be my best man?"

"Of course!" He tumbled out of the car, and I glimpsed August and Tinder's house in the background. Ari was all smiles as he appeared beside his husband, and Griffin yelled, "Get out here, guys! Mateo and Eli are getting married!"

I reached my fiancé just as half a dozen vampires crowded around Griffin and Ari, and Elias held up his phone and said, "I've got Carter and Desiree on a conference call, so we're all set." Then he waved at my phone and said, "Hi, everyone." He'd asked Carter to be his best man, and the demon looked uncharacteristically emotional as he smiled at me. It was nighttime wherever he was, while the sun was just beginning to set here in Costa Rica.

Minerva, the preacher's wife, joined us and held both phones so our friends could watch the ceremony. Elias and I stood barefoot in the soft sand, between the pretty little chapel and the sparkling blue Pacific. A laugh slipped from me, just because I couldn't contain all my joy, and as we joined hands, I said, "I love you more than anything, Eli."

"I love you too, *mi amor*." My fiancé's dark eyes crinkled at the corners as he smiled at me.

The preacher was a short, round man named Frank, who'd befriended us when we first arrived in town. He conducted a quick, sweet wedding ceremony in Spanish, with Minerva and our friends as witnesses.

I vowed to love and cherish Elias all my life, and he vowed to do the same. Then Frank smiled at us and said, in English, "What are you waiting for? You're married now, so kiss already!"

Elias and I both laughed. Then, as our friends cheered and applauded, my husband drew me into his arms and kissed me. It felt like a promise, laced with love, hope, and so much possibility.

The End

www.ingramcontent.com/pod-product-compliance
Lightning Source LLC
Chambersburg PA
CBHW061540120726
48001CB00004B/1645